6/16

RIDE AROUND SHINING

CHRIS LESLIE-HYNAN

RIDE
AROUND
SHINING

A NOVEL

HARPER

RIDE AROUND SHINING. Copyright © 2014 by Chris Leslie-Hynan. All rights reserved. Printed in the United States of America. No part of this book may be used or reproduced in any manner whatsoever without written permission except in the case of brief quotations embodied in critical articles and reviews. For information, address HarperCollins Publishers, 195 Broadway, New York, NY 10007.

Designed by Fritz Metsch

ISBN 978-0-06-228507-2

To my parents

I know that in writing the following pages I am divulging the great secret of my life, the secret which for some years I have guarded far more carefully than any of my earthly possessions; and it is a curious study to me to analyze the motives which prompt me to do it.

—JAMES WELDON JOHNSON,
The Autobiography of an Ex-Colored Man

PART
ONE

Back a few years, when you could still deny that LeBron James was the greatest player of our generation, I worked for a baller named Calyph West. He's no more than a footnote now, an already bygone figure in the true new religion of American men, the world of sports, but professional basketball is, to me anyway, the grandest distraction of them all, and know him when, why yes I did.

Remember that year, that great aberration of a year, when it seemed like all Portland was on the come-up? Before the injuries came and took us at the knees, before our city peaked and crested into caricature, when we were still young and dangerous and somehow won the West? The Heat came to town preordained to win in five or six games. It seems a half-forgotten time already, but it was the beginning of the Three Kings in Miami, so LeBron didn't have a center or a point yet, and Oden was healthy then, so it went five all right, and against all we clinched at home 4–1 after some half-anonymous man with hops and beautiful shoes denied LeBron at the rim with six seconds to go after Gerald Wallace fouled out. Yeah, that was Calyph.

That night before the trophy presentation, some national sideline guy cornered him and became the first to ask the question that'll dog him like an old sitcom actor's catchphrase into his nursing-home days: "How'd you get that high?"

Us locals knew better. "No higher'n usual," he said, tugging the flat brim of his new hat askew. It wasn't a boast. Plenty of rookies can get their elbow over the rim, but the real anomaly of Calyph's ups was their persistence, even with the brace, even after the surgery. I think we all loved him a little more for his refusal to claim the moment had brought anything special out of him.

But then, that moment never meant to him what we'd have it mean. To us, it was his promise fulfilled on the highest stage, in the crucial moment, against the best player on the planet. To him it was just a token fulfillment of what time and chance and microfracture surgery had kept from him, an extremely choice but nonetheless fleeting abatement of his hunger to matter in the games that mattered most. He was not a star; he was not ever a star. When he retired, the despair of lost promise hung about him. That there yet remained fifty long years of life with which to dissipate it could not be with any surety called good fortune. What happened to him? Among other things, I happened.

In the summer before the come-up days, when it was still all new, three tufts of smoke hung in the high air over Calyph's place, where the party was. They were pink and slightly scrawny, and looked equally like spent fireworks and signals of distress. They looked like excess, they looked like trouble, they looked like boasting and simple information. He'd just agreed on his first contract extension, and though the team wasn't bound to it yet, Calyph must have felt he had a new $32 million behind his desire to entertain. Here the party at, his smoke seemed to say. Down here, swag be phenomenal.

I could see the pink blooms from the main road, through the trees. I imagined that beneath them young men were walking between Calyph's outdoor court and his rose garden in bright suits as dapper and occasionally horrifying as the ones they'd worn on draft night, mingling with U of O guys up for the summer and our city's pittance of rappers in coral-pink topcoats and ice cream shoes, while Antonia sat high above behind a shut window like an inscrutable damsel waiting to be rescued from a distress no one could name. I'd just begun with the Wests, so I didn't know yet what I wanted more, to be down with him or up with her, and I sped toward the house in no hurry to discover it, hoping only for another day of model servitude that would worm me a little deeper into their mutual life.

I'd been watching Wimbledon when Antonia's message came, to come get her out of there. I sent back right off that it was my one day of freedom. I didn't capitalize so I'd come off angry, but of course I was pleased. All that summer I was thinking of her, and trying to spend my days off very classy. Until the weather turns, it's a good time of year for doing it up just so. You can wear a lot of nice linens that time of year. You can drink peach and pineapple juice with all your meals. In the late dusk you can walk down to Jamison Square amid gleaming new buildings with the names of old royalty, like you're on your way somewhere. It changes when the rains come, and by fall I would be sick of aspirational living and wistfulness and the simple emotions of summer. By then I'd be waiting for the wet to make the city swell with its sad, potent energy, and rot it with black moss.

Though I would come to do many things for the Wests, my official title was chauffeur. I was given an overgenerous weekly salary and the charge of an entry-level Jaguar, which I liked all the more for not being my own. I liked having to keep it mint, and I was honored and a little confused that Calyph let me garage it at my own place. Nothing in my upbringing suggested I'd enjoy a Jag a day in my life. When I was young I wasn't rich enough to have one or poor enough to want one, not with the purity of the kids who really came up from behind the scrubgrass, who could enjoy the symbol of four wheels in the driveway gleaming out harsh American success without irony. I came from the great white middle-middles, and we could enjoy nothing but our sensible lack of gaudiness, supermarket steak, and football on the weekends. This is a terrible fate, and I think I envied something about every other class of American. This envy took more than a quarter century to manifest itself, though, as from an early age I was pretty preoccupied with my own unremarkable intelligence. I more or less raised myself, with the help of a few teachers, and I quickly fixated on the shared vision of my future we created together in their cramped offices, wherein I was raised from my depressing station to theirs through the miracle of public education. When I used to hear about cars and parties, I'd tune it out with the singular focus of a young man with a wrong idea about himself. I assumed I'd arrive at the fruits of my self-denying, perpetual-student, can't-afford-it-anyway lifestyle in some kind of secondhand Corolla that smelled like acid-free paper and the absence of lust. I'd done a lot of English, and American Studies, but it was only when I discarded all that for different studies that this story begins.

I took the surface streets, because I'd been back just five weeks after two years away, and the city still glowed with the living nostalgia of homecoming—and because I wanted to make Antonia wait. Already I looked forward to rescuing her from something everyone else felt lucky to be at, picking her up out beyond the edge of the city and holding the door for her indolently, telling her no ma'am, it was no trouble at all, in the sweet, put-on voice I used to keep up the appearance of concealed bitterness. "I guess you had to come a ways," she'd say, and I'd let a sullen look flit across my face before I assured her it was not so very far. It seemed best to nurse an imaginary grudge, to mask the gratitude I felt that they'd opened their lives to me so readily.

About seven miles south of downtown Portland, along the

west bank of the Willamette, lies the Dunthorpe neighborhood. It's small and forested, and doesn't look like a neighborhood at all. Even if you find your way among the subtle hostility of sudden turns and dead ends to the properties with a river view, there isn't much to make you anticipate the homes of athletes and other young and limited gods. Most of the team lived fifteen minutes away in West Linn, just down the 205 from the practice facility, where you didn't need pink smoke to get your city friends through the politely discouraging landscape of a neighborhood designed for exceptionally chalky white people. Calyph lived next to the McCalls and the guy who invented Linux.

I pulled the car into the drive, descending from the road amid trees so tall and serene they made me want to know their names. The first sign I wasn't in a national forest was the open security gate. Just beyond it, the line of monstrous cars began. There weren't any Hummers—they couldn't be parked downtown anymore without being defaced—but there were plenty of steroidal trucks and enough black Escalades for a prince's motorcade. As the drive neared the house, the paving shifted from oil-dark blacktop to bright white gravel. The tires made a rush of white noise, a sound both antiquated and timeless. As I turned into the circle, I could almost see the ghostly grooves of carriage wheels. A woman in a vintage-store dress was sitting on the steps.

I pulled the car up alongside her, but as I slowed I saw it wasn't Antonia. She too was small and frowning, and white, but she was a northern girl, with skin like skim milk and a tattoo of a fox head on her calf. Her eyes were very blue. She was holding a cigarette in a strangely protective grip, her wrist cocked so the cherry pointed back at her. We were maybe six feet apart. The window was down between us, and we looked at one another a moment in accidental intimacy. She seemed to be waiting for a pickup, and part of me wondered if she'd just get in the car. I remember taking in the look of her mouth—her canines were slightly sharp—and feeling a strange, instinctual dislike of her, a feeling of threat, combined with the sense that if she did get in I'd accept it and drive off without a word. She'd tell me where she wanted to go and I'd ignore her, waiting for my nerves to tell me what I'd do next. All that summer I'd been having moments like that. I'd become mysterious to myself, open to everything.

She lifted the cigarette and the moment passed.

I remembered myself and felt my hand go up to my tie. "I thought you were someone," I said.

She shrugged her bare, inward shoulders. "You aren't—"

"What?" I asked.

"Someone called someone for me. A cab, I thought. But maybe it's you?"

"I'm for someone else," I said. I shut off the car and came around. "I'm for someone else," I said again and went up the steps and into the house.

Voices came from the patio in back, but the house seemed deserted. The living room was open and bright, and very beige. There were china vases and fat yellow candles and a lot of ottomans. I'd always imagined the room had been brought together with the overbearing help of an interior decorator, hurriedly chosen by Calyph's mother during his rookie season, before Antonia could veto anything. The room managed to be neither baller nor particularly livable, and I felt sure all the party guests could agree to be a little sad that some middle-aged white lady had got her way there. It'd become a known secret that Calyph wanted to buy a new place with some of his extension money, something closer to the center of the city. I'd been taking him around to see places with his mother and brother Talib, with strict orders that this operation was to be kept from Antonia, whose restlessness it was designed to appease. Still, he meant to keep this place, too, and here and there a new personality was starting to show. On one wall there was a blown-up photo of two men sitting on the stoop of a ruined Ninth Ward house, its contents tallied on the wall in red spray. A suit of armor stood in a far corner like it was ready to storm over all this fussy business.

Passing through, I came to a room I hadn't noticed before. It must have been shut up the few other times I'd been in the house. Secure in my solitude, I looked in. It was a small gallery, empty of furniture but for a cushioned bench in the center of the room. Tribal masks hung on the walls and ebony statuettes stood on pedestals. On the far wall there was a painting of a huge leaf-less tree standing isolated on the veld. It took me a second to see there was also a giant man in a black T-shirt standing perfectly still and looking at it.

He had his back to me, but I must have made some noise, because as soon as I parsed his colossal presence he turned. He was dressed in shorts and flip-flops, like a teenager headed to a pool, but he had a thick and ancient-looking beard. A friendly look beamed out of his prematurely aged face, which was familiar to me already from the billboards across town.

"That's a baobab tree," Greg Oden said.

I nodded. "Baobab," I repeated.

He turned up his palm to show me a bright digital screen. "Says here they store up to thirty-two thousand gallons of water in their trunks."

Again I nodded solemnly. From out of doors came the abrupt crack of what sounded like gunfire. Greg and I looked at one another, unsure, waiting for new sound. After a moment we heard again the far-off sound of cool talk and high laughter.

"It's probably not serious," Greg said at last.

I nodded mutely back at him once more. Putting my hands into my pockets and pivoting with a casual air, I drifted away down the hall. Somehow this didn't seem rude. There was a dreamy feeling about the afternoon that neither small-arms fire nor the sudden appearance of our city's seven-foot basketball savior could dissipate. It seemed best to float lazily along in silent witness, declining to talk to anyone, until I found Antonia.

Out back, the billboard faces were everywhere. On the patio, LaMarcus Aldridge was cooking a line of meats on a blinding grill. He too was wearing a T-shirt and ball shorts, as was seemingly everyone comfortable in their status, with only here and there a man like myself wearing a tie like a slim form of permission. Aldridge popped a bright spatula from hand to hand and called out, "Turkey burgers, turkey brats, turkey steak," in a stadium vendor's voice to no one in particular.

On a pedestal in the corner of the patio, a ten-foot ice sculpture stood gently melting in the sun, in case the casual dress should mislead anyone about the legitimacy of the celebration. She looked like a glistening Justice without her scales, sword and all, though someone had burned a hole in the palm of her empty hand to hold a blunt. She was getting freestyled to by a semicircle of guys who looked like the backfield of a college football team, though Ducks or Beavers I couldn't say. While I watched, a guy in a lavender hoodie stepped up and rapped something containing the phrase "nigga nail a bitch like a telephone pole," to general approval.

"Don't say that word," I said, under my invisible breath. No doubt the lavender halfback wouldn't care to be censured by the white help, but just five weeks with Calyph, together with my standard lifelong whiteboy fear of the n-word, had got me pretty attuned to which n's were being used organically to strengthen the patois, and which were just bad rap filler and objectionable to men of any color.

On the outdoor court, children who seemed to belong to no

one played a violent game of 21, screaming so urgently at every foul that I imagined the McCalls next door pausing on the way to the pool, shifting their grip on their blow-up rafts, and listening intently to determine if a child's murder were occurring. Joel Przybilla stood in front of the basket, looming gentle as a birch tree, softly plucking up whatever air balls came his way and redistributing the rock to the lesser children.

In the Japanese garden, a dice game was on in the raked sand. I stood on the footbridge and watched the koi pass beneath me, imagining a monk clenching his fists in outrage, yet as I came closer, the tiny, austere dice seemed an extension of the blank beauty of the landscape. Three guys in the whitest imaginable T-shirts stooped around the roller, while a man who looked like a young Julius Erving stood holding a sheaf of bills.

"You wan crap, son?"

"I'm just watching."

After a moment the roller swore and the men stepped back for him to stand. "White boy always wanna *watch*," he said. He was older than the rest, and his thick face seemed familiar.

"You fuck up my roll, white boy."

"You know you ain't used to rollin' on no cat litter, J," somebody said.

"Sorry."

"You come in here stirrin' up my chi and shit, you best roll yourself," the older man said.

"I never done it," I said, and for a second I took in nothing else, only listened to the echo of my own voice, its new, sure sound. Almost as soon as I'd come to work for Calyph I'd grown tired of my bland white talk.

"It's aight," the older man said. "Step in, I fade you."

As he dropped the dice into my palm, I placed him. He was one of the old Jail Blazers. He hadn't been with the team since the late nineties, and I couldn't imagine he lived in Portland—his most remembered remark about Oregon was the opinion that they were probably still hanging black people from trees not forty miles outside the city. If the team had known he was there they'd have sent some PR men to kidnap him, so eager were they to distance themselves from the bitterness of his misbehaving era. Now he was just a thickset, permanently angry has-been with a rap sheet, but in high school he'd been one of those black figures who entranced the suburbs with all we were not, and I'd practiced his between-the-legs dunk whenever I could find a low-enough hoop.

I knelt by the garden, rolled a seven almost immediately, got strong-armed into a double-or-nothing, and rolled another. I got up forty dollars lighter and full of the conviction that my people had been sitting in the good chairs for so long that any game that involved squatting put us at a disadvantage. Still, I felt a strange excitement in kneeling in the billow of those immaculate shirts. I remember a long gold chain brushing the back of my neck and how I shivered.

Turning back toward the patio, I was hailed to try some turkey steak, and then a new voice hollered my name, from the balcony. I heard the crack of a shot and saw a bright flash growing at me.

Something hit me in the chest and rebounded and I dropped, holding the burning place. Having never before been shot by something so bright, I rolled away from what struck me, fearing another stage, until I came up against the feet of one of the dicers standing firm. I rolled back and lay on the footbridge, trying not to writhe, as a happy chorus of profanity went up all around the yard. My body told me nothing, but I could feel in the air that I'd not been shot really, not respectably—not with a bullet or anything. Already I heard bits of muffled laughter, and after a moment's relief at the promise of more life I began to feel angry that I'd been shot by some party weapon, and was not even close enough to death to distract people from their drinks. I'd been but trifling wounded, possibly for the pleasure of the crowd, and I was left now to lie among them as a feebly trembling figure of injured dignity. If blood had suddenly begun to spurt from my chest I would've felt a certain relief. Next to me the blinding core of the flare smoked and grew small.

"Damn, son!" Calyph cried from the balcony, over the disorder. He stood at the rail, the flare gun in his hand and Antonia by his side. He had on a plain blue plaid shirt and a pair of aviators he sometimes wore like a comic prop whenever he gave me orders. I hope they soothed him; the sight of him looking down on me like an amateur dictator only stoked my hot and disoriented humiliation. Antonia looked absorbed in something some sparrows were doing in a distant place.

"You steppin' all over this place like the *Family Circus* kid," Calyph shouted down to me. "What I pay you for?"

I felt more feet around me and the dicers helped me up. As I brushed myself off, one of them crushed the flare's last embers beneath his shoe in a final gout of pink. There was a ragged hole in my shirt, just above my heart, and by the evening I'd have a quarter-sized welt I'd wish looked more serious.

I walked unsteady and stunned through the parting crowd, trying to look like my nerves were not twisted into fine fibers of hate. Once I even felt myself smile knowingly, as though this had been an elaborate practical joke we'd been planning all week to throw a little sizzle into his party. I tried to tell myself this was just a bad turn of an expected sort, that I'd fought for this sought-after job in a high-life world knowing that in its careless, loud dazzle sometimes the chauffeur got shot, for no reason at all. But seething with pride and shame, I could not sway myself from the conviction that I was less a man suffering the indignities of his job than a debased functionary of a failing empire. I felt that it was somehow correct, that I deserved it—for who can complain about being shot for being white people? And so I came under the shadow of the balcony, and looked up at this man, my master, and his wife.

"Next time, Jess, just wait with the car, okay?" Calyph had dropped his voice, but I knew it still carried to every ear that wanted to hear. "We got cameras here. We know when you're here. You don't have to call nobody. You don't have to go and look. We know. Okay?"

"Yessir," I said.

"Good. She'll be down in a second now. Next time just wait."

"Yessir."

He sniffed in a tough way, and the violence was through. "Listen, I didn't mean to hit you or nothin'. This thing always buck and shoot high."

I didn't know what to say to that, what absolution I could reasonably give. I just waved my hand a little, as if to say, Oh, did you shoot me?

He sighed, and for a moment seemed truly sorry. "Yeah. The fuck you gonna say, right? You need some Neosporin or something? A bandage? You eat?" The aviators came off, and he turned his head incrementally to include Aldridge. "Fix him up a turkey BLT real quick. Man's gotta eat."

I felt my posture relax, but the fibers of my neck were only twisted tighter by the shame of this reprieve. My nerves seethed, and it occurred to me the next time I did something wrong he'd cane me and then hand me a half-drunk lukewarm strawberry soda, to show everybody he was still a good guy.

"Maybe he want a turkey steak, Leef," Aldridge said, popping the spatula from one hand to the other with especial panache.

"What is that made-up-sounding shit?"

"Prime cut, Leef. Pure, hundred-percent prime cut turkey steak."

"Ain't nobody want that. Make Oden eat that. You leave Jess alone with that South Beach shit."

"Maybe I want it," I heard myself say.

Something in me hoped he'd rise to this, but he only turned away. "Trust me, Jess," he said a little tiredly, his voice going away from the rail. "You want that BLT."

"Yes*suh*," I said, because he'd stepped away, and would not hear.

I went off to the nearest bathroom, to raid the medicine cabinet for ointments and pain pills and hope my wound looked graver in the mirror. When I returned, an overstuffed BLT was pressed into my hand by an underling and I was made to recount my entertaining experience next to Lady Justice, who was melting unevenly in the sun.

"Coulda been worse, home," one of the rollers said. "Coulda been Jayson Williams."

"Man had the whole world."

"I been shot before," I said. I wasn't about to abide my burning just being an excuse to talk about other people who shot people. I could see Calyph coming toward us, filtering through the crowd one complicated gesture of brotherhood at a time.

"A nail gun," I said, elaborating. "BB gun, too." They did not seem impressed. "Got a fishhook in my scalp once," I added.

The men turned to me and laughed. "A real nature boy," one of them said, draping his arm around me.

"Give him a real squeeze. Shit, boy's been beat up his whole life."

Just as Calyph broke through to us at last, the man wrapped me in a full bear hug. I took a bite of BLT over his shoulder and chewed it calmly, but as Calyph came near the Justice I lowered my arm and returned the hug fully, swinging into the embrace and then out again, maneuvering the larger man toward the sculpture until I felt his shoulder strike it and then stepping free. The Justice slid easily from its pedestal, and as I watched it drop toward Calyph I felt again a slow wonder at my strange new self.

To get the job I told just two lies. It's not that I wasn't qualified. When I heard Calyph was looking for a chauffeur, I knew he wanted someone like me. It'd be just his peculiarity to want a white guy with a lot of education driving him around all "yes sir, no sir," and we had some history. I'd saved his cat.

His accident was the first I'd heard of him in almost two years. Calyph had begun to look for a driver because of a crash on Macadam Avenue, which broke his clavicle and made ESPN. The team insisted he get a driver who could ensure his safety, or they would do it for him. I was living in Michigan then, in the Upper Peninsula, finishing up my second useless degree at Northern, the only graduate school to accept me, and trying to write music reviews for whoever would take them. My old Portland boss at the restaurant delivery service sent around the job notice. The sight of Calyph's name was one of those details that recalls a gone world, as the smell of chlorine in a girl's hair relumes old summers. I think even then I read his name as a destination, a way out of a life spent looking for the wrong things in books in the terrible cold, and I relived my six memories of him instantly. There I was, toting an insulated black food bag across white stones in the cool of the evening to deliver his Evil Jungle Prince. He'd always answer the door himself, always tip at least thirty percent, rounding up to the dollar, and always use a credit card that misspelled his name as "Caleef," like it was pronounced. The year before I left Portland for grad school had been his rookie season, and he'd been the west side's most celebrated customer of Takeout Train, Inc. He pretty invariably ordered the Jungle Prince, which was milkless house curry over rice noodles—and, after not very long, his nickname with the other drivers.

My chief memory from the old days was the incident with the serval. He was the last delivery of my shift one warm June night, and when I got to the door a little white girl answered. About a month before his orders had begun including fish curries, but it was the first I ever saw of Antonia.

"Can you drive us somewhere?" she asked in a frantic voice, childlike and irresistible. She had a terrifically stylish haircut that was trying to fall over her right eye. I wasn't sure about her face at first. It's always that way with the ones who end up really mattering. She was holding what looked like an unusually long kitten with enormous ears. It was twitching its nose sluggishly and goop was leaking from one of its eyes. They'd recently bought this exotic cat, a serval hybrid, and now it was sick and refusing to eat and the only vet they knew could treat it wasn't answering the phone. It was after ten, and they didn't know what to do.

Five minutes later, all three members of the household were in the back of my Corolla, which smelled like every restaurant I'd delivered from that night. The hood would have still been dented from one of the accidents, but they were too intent on the cat to notice.

In the old days I lived down the street from a twenty-four-hour animal hospital, and I drove them there, feeling that great importance of purpose that most any urgent night errand bestows. As we sped across streetlit pools of moist night, the kitten ate a little mango sticky rice off Antonia's finger and I remember feeling relieved and unnaturally triumphant.

The cat got well. I hardly saw them again before I moved away, but when I did the tips were embarrassing. I think it was that night of impromptu chauffeuring that allowed everything to come after. I became a very minor memory, of a man who might be good in a pinch, and who knew how to get somewhere.

Even so, I knew it wouldn't be easy to get the job. Just because Calyph conducted his hiring like young money living by whim didn't mean he wasn't looking for some expertise parallel to his own. I knew, too, that there were better ways of expressing my qualifications than those that were strictly true, and that I wanted the job badly enough to use them. Why I wanted it so much, I almost couldn't say. There was a draw to the simplicity and old-fashionedness of the vocation, to being a servant almost. I got to bathe in the reflected glow of their luxury while assuring myself I was not so shallow as to actually want such things. But really it was them. If it'd been a quarterback and his blond wife I'd never have done it. It had to be a black man, exactly like Calyph in his unpredictability and buried intelligence, and his aloof and difficult white wife, his Antonia. They were like some obscure royalty, so obscure they hardly knew they were anything special themselves. To be in their lives would be the promise of a new beginning in a more vital world. Anyhow, I guess I needed the money.

When Calyph saw me turn up again, there was just enough in his attitude that I could see he wanted me to lie. When I came into his study, he was sitting behind an immense oaken desk no one his age could hope to command. It must have felt like I'd come back to him from a long way away just to be the right man for the job, and he looked relieved somehow. We shook, he offered me a seat, and then he wandered the room, whistling and inspecting its books and prestigious-looking brass items like he'd just discovered this was part of his house. There was a globe sitting on a floor stand, and he spun it slowly as he talked.

"How's your driving record?" he asked eventually.

"Spotless," I assured him.

Later he asked, with what seemed like particular interest, if I'd know how to carry myself with the dignity of one who served in a great house. "I don't want any of this humping around like a pizza boy," he explained. "Nobody got more class than a good chauffeur."

I assured him I knew this was true. Then I sat up a little in my chair and invented an explanation why.

"I came from money," I said. "We squandered it, though. I was the last of the line." The last bit was a little rich. It conjured a scene with a country house, a landscape garden—who knew what. I didn't even know what I meant, and I was afraid he would laugh and expose me. But, being nouveau himself, he nodded in perfect satisfaction.

"Y'all ever have a Bentley?" he asked.

I nodded.

"Cool, cool."

"Yeah," I said, faintly let down by his credulity.

It's not that I was ashamed of my past, exactly. My parents died young and I came up among aunts and uncles in an obsolete railroad town in Wisconsin; it was the most ordinary possible thing. When I got to college, to a school my teachers assured me was the Harvard of the Midwest, it was paid for with the life insurance money, and I found I was poorer than the people I wanted to know. Lacking even the explanation of being a scholarship kid, I just stopped talking about my hometown. My past became like one of those paper fortune-tellers, a device to be manipulated. By the time I came west and met Calyph I was pretty used to making it up anew.

The other lie was strictly necessary: of course I couldn't talk about the crashes. I knew I was sound, in spite of my priors.

Really, no one is more cautious about stopping distance than the man who's seen the highway freeze fifty feet in front of him and burst into a red nova of brake lights. No driver is really defensive until his cabin has filled with the cry of his helpless brakes, which sound like the air is full of angry metal birds.

As the Justice tipped sunward and came free of her base, I saw Calyph lift his hands and freeze, and felt my wonder chilled by a distant remorse. She had to fall, there was no way around that, and yet, having brought it off, and so neatly, I now wished myself on the other side of things. I wished I could be the one to rush forward and throw my body against the ice, to keep him safe from harm. The Justice fell with the dignity of something elemental, as if she were slipping unnoticed into some Arctic sea. She fell sword-first, and gathering his weight Calyph twisted awkwardly at the knees and sprang away as the man who'd hugged me looked over his damp shoulder, dumbfounded. She hit the ground, and I remained a moment longer to savor the crash, but instead of the million splendid shards I'd hoped for, she only cracked in two and fell into an unremarkable rubble. For the second time that hour, a cry went up among the crowd, and I saw Calyph clutch his knee, and lingered in spite of myself, to see what I had wrought. But as the men rushed to attend him, he shook it off and straightened again, joining the crowd in looking for someone to blame, and I turned quickly away amid the brief chaos and slipped into the house.

When Antonia finally came out to the car, the taste of blackened bacon stuck like ash-smear to the roof of my mouth. Brushing flecks of char from the ragged hole in my shirt, I opened the door for her with my face turned away, but she didn't get in.

"Close that," she said quietly. Then she got in the front seat.

When I had come around to the driver's side, she was still set-tling in, drawing the belt around her. She was a little one, with delicate-looking wrists and knees, and sometimes she seemed to be using a little of her concentration to keep her movements slow, so she wouldn't look like a child. Yet the effect made her seem strangely ageless, like she was younger and older than me at once.

I asked where she wanted to go and she named a clothing bou-tique in Southeast. When we'd pulled out onto the main road, I heard the pluck of her little lips pulling apart, and she said, "I'm sorry that happened."

It took me a moment to realize she wasn't talking about the sculpture. She'd turned her head a little toward me, as minutely as if she were looking in the rearview. I could only see it because one of those dangling housewife earrings I didn't like her to wear trembled a little, to announce the movement, but I didn't pay her any mind.

"You bandaged it?" she asked. "Does it still hurt?"

"I'm fine."

"Your poor shirt." She must have felt she could be tender to my wardrobe where sympathy for my actual skin would only feel like pity.

"Before people came we'd been watching that show," she ex-plained in a slow voice, finishing on a down note like that was all I'd get. She most always spoke this way, when I could get her to speak at all—with a hesitance that implied the rest of the world spoke too carelessly.

"The people-hunting show?"

She only winced. She seemed truly pained, as though no answer were possible, but then Antonia was very good at saying nothing. So often in those early days our talk was like a stoics' game, where the object was to get the other to reveal more than you. There was a tension to the game that I enjoyed as a stand-in for other tensions, and she was a worthy competitor.

"You know the one where the good chef yells at people?" she said finally. "Sort of inspires him."

I checked my blind spot, even though I knew there was no one, and turned down the air as the car shot along the leaf-darkened road.

I could see her shake her head at the edge of my eye, the earrings going off again. "He should know better than to speak to you that way, with other people around. On your day off."

"It's not my day off if you need to get somewhere," I said, giving the phrase the rich, earnest sound of a platitude. In my mind this had been the finishing volley, and I waited, swelling with humility, to be given the point. But Antonia only looked out the window and let the silence take us.

"Madame didn't enjoy the party?" I asked, after we'd driven awhile.

I stole a glance and saw her small mouth compress. Her lips had a loose look for one who spoke so rarely, like they'd be supple if you bit one. She was always twitching and pursing them, and making little moues.

"Madame," she said, like a curse.

Her mouth seemed to have an active life of judgment all its own. At first I hadn't liked this, thinking that behind her reserve she was censuring everything by some merciless private code. At any moment I thought the barely parted lips would shrivel in disdain and I wouldn't know why. Eventually they did, but it was only rarely, and most always correctly, so that even when she looked the picture of a snotty little rich girl, I agreed with her, and approved.

"I'm sorry you had to come all the way down here so I could shop," she said.

"It's not so very far," I assured her.

"I know I said I wouldn't. It must be a pain, to be sent for like that."

"It's a pleasure to be sent for like that," I corrected her.

As we swept briefly onto I-5 past Ross Island, a semi tried to get into an accident with us. We wanted the next exit, and instead of braking for the truck I sped up while dodging left, got in front of him, then slid right across two lanes while falling beneath the speed of traffic to make the exit. I didn't think Antonia had noticed until we nosed toward MLK and she said, "You're a good little driver," with a snap in her voice.

"Yes, Miss Daisy."

"Is there anywhere you'd like to go after we're done?" she teased.

She made it sound like I'd want a soft-serve cone. But I felt the proximity of her small knees, imagined the backs of them damp from the heat of the day, pressed together now and drying in the cool of the car, and could think of no reply.

After her shopping, she had me stop alongside Laurelhurst while she rolled a cigarette. It takes a special upbringing to need to be driven to a park in order to light up, but one of the first things I'd learned about Antonia was that she'd come from southern money, and that it made her both worldly and impossibly young. She'd met Calyph at Carolina. During the summer before her junior year, she took a tour of Europe with her mother, on a boat—they went up and down the Rhine and all the way around through the Strait of Gibraltar. Yet apart from her years in Chapel Hill and her travels, she'd led an exclusively suburban existence, going from daughter to housewife at twenty-two. One night I'd taken her to a dinner for the players' wives, and she'd asked me if a tag on a Pearl District warehouse meant there was a lot of gang activity around there. In the next block we'd passed a Chilean art gallery and a Scandinavian bar that advertised their digestifs and herbal liqueurs.

"That's where they go to talk truce," I explained, and she muttered a little under her breath in a muted, rambunctious growl that seemed aimed largely at herself. After dinner she went back there and had a drink with Sergio Rodriguez's wife. "They wouldn't serve me a julep," she reported in an awed voice.

"Have you got anything new for me to listen to?" she asked now, as we drove north. "That last just sounds like that electronica music."

I gave her the bale eye for a second before I realized she was tweaking me. She'd learned about my music writing from Calyph and had started asking for copies of what I liked. She said she was buying them on vinyl if she liked them, too, and although I hadn't seen proof, I imagined I was contributing to a largely decorative library somewhere in some unseen room of their house. She'd have to put something on, occasionally—she'd hop on a treadmill to *Lift Your Skinny Fists Like Antennas to Heaven!* and then stand before the mirror, removing a sweat-laced bandanna and feeling, through the aching in her calves, that those screwdrivered guitars stood for something she'd once thought essential, some closeness to a young urban struggle she'd felt sensitive to before she'd moved here to be with Calyph and lost it again among the lawns.

I think she'd tried to like music for a while, probably in college, and then lapsed. All our college ideals, our moods and exultations, you couldn't take them seriously now. But the ideals of the past that make us curse aloud in shame just to remember them are the same ones that, another day, in different weather, somehow stand up and become serious again, become the vital parts of better people we could have been, lost along the road, and, I'm saying, she had asked me for music like it was important to her this way. It was like she thought it would free her from her sterile suburban distance and connect her again with some lost essence that coursed hidden from her through the streets of the real city. Sometimes she'd give me vague directions to drive around an unexplored quadrant, and look out the window like she was hoping we'd bump into everything she missed. But she was too proud to tell me what she was looking for, to feel the ridicule of saying "Take me to the *real* city," and I was glad of it, because I was looking for that same place myself, and wouldn't have known where to go.

I sometimes had the sense that she was familiar with me, and flirted with me even, because she thought we had some particular, indefinable thing in common. It wasn't the blue-blooded stuff—I was always worried she was going to see right through that. It was a white thing, somehow. I lived in the city, I knew about records, and I was taciturn enough to appear fashionable. I felt the whole of her faint interest in me came out of these things. What drew me to her world was one of the very things that discontented her about it: the dearth of people like me. She turned to me like a confidant from the distant world of whiteness and leafed through me like a hipster primer, not knowing how poorly I would prepare her for that world.

As we turned up Thirty-Third, she began to roll herself another cigarette, and for a moment the sweetish smell of the tony old stuff filled the car. "That smells like my uncle's *Wall Street Week* tobacco," I said.

She eyed me with a brow up. "His what?"

"He had a pipe. But he'd only smoke it on Friday nights, during *Wall Street Week*."

"My dad watched that show," she said. "Great-Uncle Bobby taught Louie Rukeyser at Princeton."

I felt enamored of these names, yet irritated by them, too. I couldn't believe she couldn't hear how she sounded. "Louie and Great-Uncle Bobby," I repeated witheringly. "Louie and Great-Uncle Bobby played Diplomacy in the study at Fort Nancy," I said, clipping each of the words.

She eyed me like I was acting crazy, and the talk died once more. We snaked through the streets of old, elegant neighborhoods I only knew as whorls on maps, and she tucked her cigarette into a flowered metal case.

"I used to wish I'd gone to Princeton is all," I said at last, just to get it behind us.

"No you didn't," she said decisively. It was like this was common knowledge among all the informed people of the Eastern Seaboard.

"A couple of my uncles went there," I said. "The last of our money."

She snickered. "Do we have to start on that today? The ongoing saga!"

Her voice broke out scathing, softened by laughter but not much. It did that sometimes, became exuberant or savage from out of a perfect composure—it had pounce. She laughed to herself, delighted at her own rudeness, her little jokes. When she saw I wasn't amused her little hand flashed out at me for a moment, and I thought she was going to cup my face and cry "Poor baby," or maybe flick my ear or something. Her little wrists flashed at me between the seats, wanting to be grabbed.

"If the missus finds my history tedious . . . " I began, thinking how easy it would be. I'd been provoked; it was Sunday; it wouldn't be out of line.

"The missus?" she laughed. "Last time it was madame. Can't keep your shit straight at all."

Taking the wheel firmly with one hand, I watched my other

shoot out and snatch one of her wrists, then seek on for the other. Still laughing, incredulous now, she twisted away from me instinctively, but when she brought her free hand up to pull my fingers off her wrist, I grabbed that, too. Having hold, I said nothing, but only sat up straight and drove calmly on, my face stern, showing her how adults behaved.

She too said nothing, only squirmed against me in silence. Massing her strength to pull away, she grunted in exertion, a fabulous noise. Failing, she pulled her wrists in, against the bare skin of her chest, into the light-boned valley of her. I'm sure she thought I'd let her off then, but I didn't feel compromised. With another low noise, she bucked and dipped her head, and I felt the brush of her hair against my hand. Seeing a light go yellow in front of us, I told her to look out, and for a moment before she wrenched free I felt against the delicate skin of my wrist the teeth of this feral girl.

We sat at the light in a swollen silence, breathing. The back of my wrist was damp. I tried to force my face to go blank again, to become that droop-lidded, expressionless face of servitude I'd practiced before the mirror, pleased at its classical look. She massaged her wrists and returned a strand of hair to its right place.

I'd made up my mind about her face by then all right. At first I'd thought it was just her stature, the star's wife with her exclusive girlhood, that it was all secondhand desire and conquest and snobbery, although God knows she seemed normal enough. And some star—that flare-gunner didn't even start. She was sweating then, just a little gleam around the temple, but it brought out her curious, unbeautiful face from beneath that haircut that looked like half a week's salary. Her nose was a little thin, a little prominent; her lips were thin. It was something her neighbors might get worked on, but she wasn't the type. Hers was a face that time would scarcely age, and I thought for how many years she'd look almost as girlish as that. If she had work she'd have to watch it fall apart. She didn't need it, after all: her eyes were like the ocean on a bad day, her thin mouth was wet and full of dry laughter, anyone would want to throw one into her narrow body, through her inscrutable judgments and her little bones.

She was looking at me strangely. "I'm sorry I taunt you," she said. Her voice was flat, almost perfectly detached, yet I felt I could hear a husk of emotion beneath.

"I don't mind it."

"But you do," she said. She needn't have said that. I knew she knew, that I was hurt somehow to mix up these words.

"I'm sorry if I don't act like you're used to," I said, surprised by the wounded hauteur in my own voice.

"I'm sorry you think I want you to."

We passed another park and I glanced over, very businesslike, like maybe children were lining the road there, waiting to leap into traffic. Some rockabillies were playing kickball.

"Why'd you really send for me today?" I asked.

Her eyes roved slow over my face. "That's not your business, boy," she said lightly. "Make a left at the next light."

We came up on Alberta, a street the suburban myths of my first driving days held to be in the ghetto, and now a center of white return. All over North Portland, no corner market could breathe easy, no barbershop was safe from the visionary gentry. At first these places were just built up around, so they could stand as symbols of authenticity, but when the disharmony became deafening they'd give way, to become impractical boutiques. Going west toward the new development blocks, I watched the old, worn-down taco stands fade in anticipation of the gleaming new taquerias.

"You live in a place like this?"

She asked like she was sure, and I didn't contradict her. But in seeing these blocks through her eyes, the parodic figure of the concerned gentry, marching around with its dogs, supporting local businesses, looking at black people being poor and feeling responsible and putting on troubled faces as if to say, get off that stoop and do something noble so I can rejoice in your humanity— these figures faded, and then I couldn't deny that the place was beautiful, flush with the transitory luster of young money and relatively new ideas. She smiled wistfully at a sidewalk crowd waiting for brunch seats at that incongruous hour and I realized that here was her real city, that she'd found it already without me. Perhaps it could even stay this young forever, and we could all get together and march against the police or something, and eat barbecue, vegan barbecue, forever free from our histories.

I felt my failure of comportment recede a little under the pleasure of arbitrary judgments against whole neighborhoods, and watched Antonia's face gleam in the summer light.

"See?" she said. "This is the place. Why would you want to act like you live anywhere else? You're never going to have to meet my father."

"Maybe I will," I said. I could see myself shaking his hand, decorous and restrained, a self-made man.

We found the block she wanted and turned off into the side streets. She pointed me to a stop. I executed a fairly gorgeous Y-turn-into-parallel, and we parked on the other side of the street.

"You can shut it off," she said.

We sat in front of a narrow, brightly colored house. The porch rails were striped vivid as candy, and leaning forward to look past her I could see there were new, bright flowers in the beds. The house looked too clean. The walk was freshly swept, the porch was bare, and the blinds on the windows were all drawn up exactly halfway.

She didn't say anything. She just sat there, her hands cupped quietly in her lap, looking at this house. I was surprised: I'd been driving Calyph to condos and lofts. This looked like the bright, attractive home a young couple might buy after getting minor promotions at their respective nonprofits and deciding they were ready to settle down and invest in a reason to start attending community meetings. And then, once again, my derision faded, and it was just a little house in the city, a bit cute for my style, but a place two people could live well in the shadow of its quaint impoverished history and fragrant old trees. I could see us there, renting the place, moving around inside behind the blinds on some afternoon like this, on the kitchen table or just only talking, as the summer air poured through the windows and the city went on around us, happy and unnoticing.

"Didn't even take the flyers out yet."

"What?" I asked.

She opened her door. Stepping onto the sidewalk, she bent over a Realtor's sign I hadn't seen. She lifted the door of the plastic box on the signpost and took out all the flyers. The hooks on the bottom of the sign were empty, the house's status unknown. She held the flyers out for me to see as she came back to the car.

"It was supposed to be a secret," I said.

"What was?" she asked, and I felt a sort of chill of understanding go over me.

"This house."

"It is," she said.

Antonia was determined to be as remote from her husband's festivities as possible, and had me leave her behind on Alberta—to have dinner with a friend, she said. She wanted a pickup at nine, and I ended up back at my own place for a few hours.

All the latter half of that year I was subletting from an old bachelor who lived in the sprawling attic of a semidilapidated Victorian up near Forest Park. He was not, properly speaking, that old—a retired teacher of some soft subject, in his late fifties, gone to Alaska for the rest of the year—but in absentia he became each day a purer amalgam of his checkered ties, folded white socks, and all-too-vivid décor. His apartment was home to a number of curiosities. The narrow walls of the stair leading up to the apartment were papered with old concert posters and ads for Mexican wine. Mardi Gras beads hung everywhere in the kitchen, over things that seemed to want no adornment—the knob on the stove's exhaust hood, and the smoke detector.

I made a dinner of canned gumbo in his rusting galley kitchen and took it into the front room to eat. The room was like a plaintive advertisement for literacy. The high table was stacked with books almost exclusively on the subject of love, and the coffee table was lined inches deep with old newspapers from everywhere—I put my bowl on a yellowing copy of *Le Monde*. Maybe the look and smell of old newsprint just fired the bachelor's tepid, remembering blood, but the whole place seemed to be awkwardly waiting for something. Like the unused candles in Calyph's living room, the room appeared partially a pose, a display of moldering erudition he'd set as carefully as a trap and then had to live amid, season after season. It was as though he was just waiting for some woman to come up his groaning stair and turn the corner and say, "Why, look at all these beautiful *books*." Her face would become suffused with kindred light, and he would be a bachelor no longer.

But, God, he put himself all out there. It was his home, and it was his right, and I was just a stranger paying to be there, but I felt like every day I lived there I was leafing through his loneliness. Every time I put down a glass of water, it seemed like I might watermark his soul. A woman would have to displace six solemn artifacts of his heart just to sit down in that place. Sometimes I'd look up, at the photographs of his parents and the pencil-sketched self-portraits and the watercolor nude he'd painted himself, and it seemed his too-open heart itself hung on the wall among them, its ventricles sloughing in the exposure.

When I liked being a servant, it was because it gave me a code that demanded I not be like the bachelor. Your heart is your own, it said, now never show it. Plant it in a dark room, in rich soil, where it will age well and grow so wine-dark and full no nail will ever hold it to a wall. When I made improvements to my past, and even when I took liberties within my work, I felt what I said and did were not wrongs, because they were all done in fidelity to my new buried heart. The thing was growing in bulges. Strange new shoots were flying out of the earth, and I had to accept them and tend to them even when they came in strange guises and surprised me. When I felt I ought to grab Antonia, or tip that sculpture over, I knew I must go through with these things, in spite of their danger, lest in denying this new energy mine should shrivel back again into a lackey's heart, as dry and small as a walnut carried around in an old paper sack. I didn't mean to cause them any real trouble.

When I brought her home the status cars were all departed, leaving great ruts at the edge of the drive. We went over the blacktop and onto the gravel and I saw the house was dark but for the debris: there was an inexplicable mound of popcorn on the apron of the garage, and on the front steps a few discarded beer bottles lay gleaming greenly in the moon.

Antonia had gotten a flower from somewhere and twined it in her hair, and coming from her dinner she looked beautiful, and the flower looked somehow flagrant. She seemed full of health, as though she'd drunk a lot of special juice and washed her face in a bowl of rainwater. The flower was a blue, open, fleshy-looking thing, and I remember feeling that she ought to take it out from there, that it was immodest. The stem rested above her ear, and, turning back to her now in the moonlight, I saw the faintest line of residue running down her neck where a drop of water had trickled out and dried.

She gave a prefatory cough and handed up one of the Realtor's flyers from that afternoon. "That house you saw," she said.

"Yes?"

"The papers are all signed."

I didn't know whether I ought to act surprised. I thought maybe some rich old phrase was required of me.

"Many congratulations," I said.

"Thanks. It's a long time coming."

"When will you start there?"

"Oh, soon."

"Having servants?"

"Servants," she repeated lightly. "It's too small for that. Besides, I think Calyph will be staying up here most the time."

There was a pause in which I pretended to examine the flyer. "Congratulations once again," I said. My voice sounded dead somehow, like the car was filtering vital things out of the air.

I could hear her dress slide along her skin as she leaned forward, and then her voice was just behind my neck. "I hope you'll show me more of the city," she said. "Now that you know how to get me there." Her voice seemed poised exactly at the edge of open flirtation and simple appeal; like the flower, it was innocent and indecent all at once.

"Of course," I said, and for a second I let my hand slip from the wheel, so I could take it again in a strong new grip. "I bet it was a long party. You ought to see how Mr. West is feeling."

"He's probably not even here," she said.

The dark house sat before us, inviting. I could walk through all the rooms without turning on any of the lights, and see their night stillness. "He said something the other day . . . ," I began vaguely.

"What?" I turned off the car then, and her voice was sharp in the new silence. She sounded forced out of comfort.

"Maybe we could go inside," I said.

"I don't think that's . . ." But she couldn't decide what it wasn't. I heard her belt click and release.

"We're comfortable in here," she said, reassuring herself. "Say what you have to."

I felt my lips press together. Suddenly it was me the silence encroached on. I turned the key and the music came quietly back. "The house," I said. "He doesn't even know you're looking."

"No," she said at last. "He'll know soon," she amended feebly. "I just want to surprise him."

"You better surprise him before he surprises you."

She didn't say anything to this, and I didn't look at her, but somehow her confusion was apparent. There was some kind of awkward beat.

"I've been taking him around to see Realtors, for when the extension goes through," I said. "It's been kind of a thing for him. You're not supposed to know."

"Oh," she said.

When she spoke again, her voice had changed once more. I couldn't tell if it was sheer caprice or if she was trying to buy me, but again her voice warmed, husky and irresponsible. "I suppose you could come inside a minute," she said. "Have a coffee for the drive."

I made an indifferent noise. "What kind you got?" I asked scornfully.

"Hot," she said.

"I bet you make a thin cup," I told her.

"Oh?"

"Your cream is skim," I declared.

In the kitchen I watched the fuzz at the back of her neck glow under the lights of the exhaust hood. She was still wearing her flower, and I wondered if I held her head very still while I squeezed the stem, would any juice come out. She was working at some new apparatus that reimagined the future of coffee so you loaded the grounds one plastic bullet at a time. The sounds hissed and roared through the silent house.

My cup was made in thirty seconds, and then Antonia's phone rang and she turned away with her finger up and wandered off. From the dark of the dining room I heard her brightly laughing. I stood there a minute, feeling neglected, and then angry with myself that I should so easily miss her.

I took to the family room, and until my eyes adjusted to the moon-shaded black I moved among the ideas of their things. I gripped the edge of a couch, and though its grain felt as ordinary as anything from my own childhood, in the dark it could've been any couch in any room where I felt out of place and privileged to be. In the dark, things I might have scorned elsewhere as Mc-Mansion set pieces felt owned and earned. The fat candles I'd elsewhere thought tacky were cool and timeless to the touch, and felt like all the surfaces in all the rooms where I'd stood as a young man and sensed that here was a place that led to other places where life sloped alluringly out of my reach. In the dark I remembered the bright stone paths of the old summer places on Lake Geneva, down which the wet footprints disappeared, and every threadbare hall outside the apartment of an indifferent woman—every place that was that place that was as far as I would get. I was always finding those rooms, places where a middle-middle man would stall out until he had matured or risen or simply become better. And hadn't I? I was a man of action now, I assured myself. I shaped destinies.

I picked a curio off the mantel, the skyline of the Chapel Hill campus done out in copper and encased in glass, and turned it around in my hands, feeling again the mystery of why I'd come to work here. To be near to Antonia's life was to be surrounded by all the old, passed-down desires I'd taken up with young hands, ten years ago or more, in the initial creation of what I thought to be my eternal personality. She was a campus spire and a cool, judgmental charisma and my torn cover of *This Side of Paradise*. Now I was in the dark among her airs and her blue-blooded things, and as they grew gradually visible around me I knew I was helpless to judge them as harshly as they deserved—they'd become fundamental to my aspiration. She herself was a person and not a symbol, but the relics of her childhood, her Italian swimwear catalogs and her damp upper lip, those belonged to everyone who grew up in a nowhere junction town dreaming our erotic, limited, and endless American dreams.

In the half-light of the dining room, she stood silent with the phone at her ear, a fading amusement on her face. When she saw me, she dropped the phone an inch or two and looked at me with her expression suspended halfway into apology. She had seen what was on my face and it had made her wary.

I stood near and she did not step back and I took her upheld wrist and moved it away. I put my hand through her hair, around her ear where the flower was. Her eyes were very large, she was frightened, and I kissed her. Her mouth was so small a careless man could miss it. I tested the pull of her lips; they were not so loose as I had thought. She did not respond, nor pull away, and after what must have been at most five seconds I leaned back and took the flower slowly from her ear.

She hadn't put down the phone, and as she felt the flower go she resumed the conversation as though she'd been pulled away from it only a moment by some trifling necessity.

"You're kidding," she said into the phone. "What?" She looked slightly shaken, but she smiled at me a little, chidingly. Then she turned away.

I was on my way out when I heard him dribbling. I knew he'd been around somewhere. It was a low, flat sound, and when the ball struck there was a finality to it, like each time was the last time it would ever land. I stopped in the hall and waited to hear the sound again.

When it came, I took my cup out across the patio and onto the narrow paved path toward the court. One half of the court was bright with floodlights, but the lit key stood empty. At first I thought he was chasing an errant ball into the murk, but I heard the ball go through the far net twice and he didn't appear. He was playing on the dark half.

I laid down the cup and crept around the spill of light to the near corner. I crouched a moment with my fingers resting in the mesh of the fence. He must have been so focused inward I needn't have bothered being afraid he'd see me. Even before I could see him, I knew he was trying to figure something out about himself, testing his first step—I could hear the asphalt grind as he pivoted and then tried to explode. He always took one dribble, and it was the loudest sound. He'd lay up and then catch the ball out of the net and walk back slowly and go again. The calm of this walk unsettled me—it was like he was taking his time to get feedback from all his sinews and nerves.

After a couple dozen drives, he stopped and I heard the ball slam down with what seemed a satisfied sound. I could see him dimly then, the ball under his foot, and he raised his arms and detached something from himself and it sailed toward me and fluttered to the ground. I caught the smell of sweat then, and it threw me. I'd never smelled his sweat before. It smelled the same as mine, and this offended me. Until they get televisions that smell, ballers are people who have pure water running off them as a byproduct of their elegance, and sweat is the thing the rest of us make as we feel ourselves fall short. Sweat was what came off our slick freckly skin and hung in our ugly socks as we breathed hard in endless games of three-on-three in decrepit gyms while our women looked sadly on as our layups rolled off. Calyph smelled harsh as a wet woman does, to shame the hopes of small men who wish for a perfect world where everything good is fragrant.

With his shirt off, he rippled and glistened in the moon, and I began to feel uneasy. He broke from the rigidity of his drills, and just shot around, and I saw the contour of him, and tried to make out his tattoos. Really it's white people who should be doomed to smudgy, half-invisible tattoos—it would suit us better. I told myself I'd sneak away once I made out the single word that was written on his back in script, between the shoulder blades, but he would not stay still. I watched and watched the ink on his body in the dark, and when I looked away at last I saw I'd pulled the flower all to pieces.

(3)

Driving out to Dunthorpe in the early morning, with the roads still clear and dew on the medians, I liked to think of the players in their houses spread out over the city. Year by year it just gets easier to see all America spread naked under the sky. If you want to see what kind of car Michael Jordan's chauffeur is driving these days, you can just find the latest high-res satellite photograph of Highland Park and blow it up until you see the two Bentleys, black and white, sitting in his drive like pixilated Matchbox cars. I liked to think of someone finding the coordinates to Calyph's house on a message board somewhere, like you can with MJ. As I drove past the early dog walkers and spry old men dutifully following ancient health advice, I imagined all of Portland unfolding that same way on those mornings, when the mist cleared and all our lives stood open to a glimpse from the satellites and the street views. Somehow the city was more alive to me with the team spread across it, humming with the energy of their half-hidden lives, from the glittering mistresses' apartments in the Lloyd District to the sturdy exurban mansions of West Linn, built on rolling hills of grass seed. In satellite photographs, we were together.

At Calyph's, I sat at the kitchen island and looked down at the laptop I'd been instructed to bring as though it were a mixing board or a ten-key, some kind of byzantine machine.

"What am I doing here again?" I called out.

"You know about cars," Calyph shouted back vaguely.

In front of me sat a fresh copy of *The Oregonian* and a stack of pricing guides tagged from the central library. I guess I was looking for a deal on a used car. I felt odd about being in their house again. There was no sign of Antonia, but after the previous night I preferred to be kept at a formal distance from their real lives for a little while.

"Look up Lost Boys Staffing while you at it," Calyph said, leaning against the door frame. "Gonna fill things out here with a houseman in a bit, hook him up with this old ride. There's a brochure for 'em around here somewhere. Make y'self at home, too," he said, tilting his head toward the living room, and went off down the stairs.

I got up and settled down again in a deep, stiff chair. I didn't see any brochures, but a pretty clunky-looking Web page told me Lost Boys was a charitable venture started by Joseph Jones, one of the league's more august veterans. He'd won a championship with the Pistons, but he was in his twilight now, known as much for being a respected locker-room figure and having the league's most dignified beard as for the workman's rebounding and post defense, which were all he had left to give to the hardwood. Off the court he always wore spectacles and cream-colored suits, a true Georgetown warrior-scholar. According to the site, after Jones won his ring he'd replaced his staff with new servants he'd found through a company that trained resettled refugees from Sudan and the Congo. He'd later invested in the company, becoming its emissary to the league and eventually its figurehead. The site went on vaguely about its nonprofit status before boasting that all the staff were trained to drive and, later, helped to purchase cars.

Jones's own staff was a handsome five-person affair. Each man looked like a consummate professional, dapper and severe in his cream-colored livery, and among this proud lineup I couldn't help note the presence of a chauffeur, distinguished by his driving cap. It seemed a praiseworthy venture but I wasn't about to be pushed out by some humanitarian cause.

Finishing with the site, I got up again to wander. A cloud shoal was rolling in, and a little mist was crawling across the lawn. Behind glass there was no way to tell it wasn't already fall. Out in Illinois, the bright, discouraging gate with "23" on it must still be baking beneath the sun and the satellites, but all across western Oregon the mists were gathering, limbering up for their six-month stay.

Turning from the window, the room seemed charged with the changing of seasons, and I wondered how Calyph and Antonia's life had flowed through it. They must not have always avoided the formal living room as a stiff and superfluous place—there must have been a time when, twenty-one and trying to own all these things for the first time, they'd put their feet up on all the ottomans and turned all the throw pillows around slowly in their hands and thought, what a lot of underfoot shit comes with an adult house, and how incredible that we'll come to find it all crucial.

I'd expected the fireplace to be gas, but it held four pieces of quartered, fragrant birch. I knelt down in front of it, on a throw. I let my fingers sink into the weave and couldn't but think of them there, in front of the fire together at a long day's end. I saw one of the logs popping in the tentative southerner's fire he would've made, and the ash thrown up against the glass. He covers her, instinctively; the back of his young neck gleams in the golden light. Her startled toes curl into the rich fibers.

I felt the urge to lie down, and then from nowhere I heard a human voice meowing. It was a lithe, expressive sound—neither embarrassing nor embarrassed. I heard the stairs taking weight and crouched low against the couch. She meowed again, searchingly. The sound fell and then rose, just as if she were calling his name.

I heard her walk behind me into the hall. There she paused, and meowed again, twice. This time her meows seemed to have a serious, French sound. "Miau, miau," they rang, assertive and frustrated. It wasn't cutesy; she was too fluent. She went down into the basement.

I rose in a rush and lightfooted it back to the kitchen. So that was the language that gave expression to her elusive heart. When left alone, looking up the river at the distant city lights, did she yowl? Did she purr when she felt her underwear being pulled down across the backs of her calves? Pulling out my pen, I began to wildly circle things in the classifieds.

After about five minutes, I heard them come back up the stairs. His voice lashed out deeply with a strong, playful sound, and in his pauses I could hear a murmured response.

She was first up the stairs. I thought I'd turned my face away, but somehow I saw her. She was wearing baby-blue pajamas, and there was a sheen of sweat on her face as though she'd been exercising. She seemed to take in my presence, lower her eyes, lift them back up again defiantly, and walk around the corner all in one unbroken motion. Calyph merely glanced at me, in skeletal exasperation, and one of his hands flashed up as he followed her out into the rest of the house. I couldn't tell if the flash was a *You think you supposed to look at this*, a *Now we got to have a lady problem*, or just a *Yeah, she meow*.

I heard her on the stairs again, and then Calyph's voice. "What? Just 'cause you—? Aw, he don't matter!"

Of course she didn't answer him, and I tried to picture the aggrieved expression on her face.

Then he was coming at me down the hall. His eyes were

almost closed, so I could only see a glimmer between the lashes, and he had Antonia by the wrist as she slid along behind him. I waited, my heart beating up. I thought if my shirt stuck to me they'd see it beating.

"How you doin' with that?" Calyph demanded.

"Good," I said. "Well."

"You find anything for a compact yet? Civic or something?"

"I've got a couple. A nice Mazda. We'll have to run the VINs," I said, straining for some kind of evenness in my voice.

"Good. Do that." Calyph turned to her and released his grip. "See? He's doin' his work."

"I'm sure," she said huskily.

"So why can't we be? Why can't we be just as we please?"

She shook her head derisively at this naïveté, and his eyes bugged a little back at her in frustration.

"We can be natural when Mom's here," he said. "When Leeb's here. So why not him? And don't give me that *they family*, 'cause you know you don't think so. I mean, what are we paying this man eight hundred a week for if we can't—"

But he couldn't finish. The look in her eyes routed him. It was that look of a woman asserting that a man is not seeing something obvious. Her sensitivity was greater than his, it said, and to keep on like this was only to risk more disdain for all in him that was lagging and blind.

Without breaking her gaze, Calyph tilted his head a little and said, "Hey Jess, you think you can give us a little meow?"

"What," I said.

"I mean, if it don't offend you. I'm not tryin' to use you. I ain't tryin' to belittle. Just wondered if you might give us a little meow."

I coughed back in my throat, and it seemed to echo in the taut quiet.

"Don't you," she whispered. And I knew then that I'd have to. Otherwise it was the two of us opposing him, and I couldn't allow anything like that.

I knew I had to spin the sound somehow, or it'd come out like a pitiful, forced thing. I imagined a man sitting in the back room of a restaurant, his hands on a checked cloth, tilting back his chair, flushed with power and an acceptable meal and the respect of the street. He brushes the backs of his fingers over his chin, and—

"Meow," I said, shrugging.

"Meow," Calyph repeated, in a reasonable tone. His whole posture was bent to his wife in appeal. His hands were cupped together.

Now she looked really furious. Her whole face was flushed, the tips of her fingers bloodless where she gripped her thighs through the thin cotton.

I don't know what he saw in her that told him her anger was endangered. But suddenly he smiled at her very carefully. "Errbody meows," he said wisely.

Her lips moved at him in silent fury.

"Don't everybody meow, Jess?"

"Everybody *I* know," I said.

We watched the flush creep down her neck. "You are the fucking—"

She turned suddenly, lithe and alive and faking the fury now. Before she could avert her face I saw the severity straining to hold. With the cuss she'd forgiven us, and now she had to book it before she laughed and lost all face.

"You are the princes," she said savagely, going away. We listened to her footsteps recede.

"Oh, where my kitty cat, where my kitty cat?" Calyph sang softly. It was the first moment of brotherhood I'd felt with him since the day he hired me. My nerves tingled, as with a flush of some golden liquor. I had to struggle not to grin like a boy. I felt my face slowly go still, and the self-mastery gave me a second flush of strange ecstasy—I felt my face glowing behind the mask.

It wasn't until that day that I ever understood them together. While I kept my eyes down and pretended to work, I watched them at rest and at play. I got up to get a glass of water and sat back where I could get a good angle of them. Antonia was still wearing her pajamas, but I wasn't so concerned with watching her in them. She could have been asserting her rights, or daring me to find the line of her terry underwear, but I just wanted to be sure they couldn't go off and have some moment together behind a wall where I couldn't see.

Calyph got up and put a record on. I'd noticed the turntable before—it was one of the few items on the main floor of more than token quality, and I envied it, because back in the Midwest I'd had a much lesser version of the same. I knew his taste went beyond the blunt mainstream rap I assumed of most athletes—the stuff I used to hear swelling the glass on aptly named Suburbans in the parking lots of once-segregated fraternities. But when he put on Pavement on blue vinyl, that was a little past my expectations.

"Ice baby," he sang. "I saw your girlfriend, and she blah blah lo-fi singer, why won't you let me hear?"

Antonia snorted.

"What? I put it on, didn't I?" He leaned out to catch my eye, his voice carrying easily through the rooms. "This was the first record she gave me in college. This was the music that was gonna bridge all our gaps."

"You like it," she said dismissively.

"Sure I like it. Remember back when making music on the cheap was a big art movement? The culture was like, shit yes, white people finally made some tinny sounds for us."

"Did you get her something back?"

Calyph looked quickly away.

"*Fear of a Black Planet*," he said at last.

"He wanted me to know who he *was*," Antonia said, drawling.

I heard a noise on the stairs, and Antonia whistled and clapped her hands. The serval ran into view, chirping, and lay down at Calyph's feet. He rubbed it with rough affection, as if it were a dog. "How'd you get aloosed?"

The serval was interrogated about its day, and lay there wide-eyed, as if listening intently for some distant sound far beyond the trivial noises of its feeders. It had huge ears like lacrosse pockets, and its alertness made it seem a living mechanism for sensing far-off danger. Every few minutes some inaudible provocation would stir the creature, and it would go trotting swiftly out of the room. "Siren goin' off," Calyph would call after it.

After it came back the first time, Antonia brought it over to me and reintroduced it as though to an old benefactor. Her manner showed no shadow of the previous night, and I was glad. I worried he would notice any change, and for the time being I was just glad to get a taste without upsetting anything. Siren was a savannah, technically, smaller than a true serval but about twice the size of an ordinary house cat, with limbs like a giraffe's. It butted at Calyph's knees while he stood to take a call, eighteen feet of legs between them.

Most any time somebody called Calyph on the phone, he seemed to step out of our polite, muted world and into somewhere far away. The phone made him street again, and he had the self-possession to go there, to make no concession to the fact that while he was talking twice as loud and half again as fast, and ending an impressive percentage of his sentences with freshly coined insults, he was still standing on plush carpet looking out through lace curtains at something people might yet want to call a greensward.

Meanwhile, Antonia, paying him no mind, went calmly on, cutting from a magazine with a pair of nail scissors.

It wasn't the first time I'd seen them so. I remembered standing by their door in the food-delivery days, the curry-smelling food bag at my feet. He was gone to get her card; she must have insisted on paying that night. We had some complicated system if you didn't pay cash—they gave the numbers over the phone and then we had to see the card again and take a rubbing on carbon. I always did it with the side of a pen with the name of my college on it, so they'd know I was a man of promise.

Antonia was tinkering with something on a laptop. She was deep into it, and he had to put a hand on her shoulder before she looked up. She brought up the card, a little annoyed at the interruption, but polite, trying not to lean her mood onto me, while he got a call. He walked back and forth, in and out of view into rooms I hadn't yet seen. You could tell he was talking to some old homeboy. His voice had changed, and the old hood slang was brought alive to enrapture the beige sofas with its complexity and sure cadence.

They seemed so separate there, each with their own incompatible histories, which their marriage had bound together. Her cool hands were clicking away, buying this, matching that shade to another shade, contributing to an election campaign, who knew what, and then she came forward, while he strode around, getting the updates. "That Nutella motherfucker?" he'd said incredulously. It was the same now, only she was cutting, and it was some other man he was dubious of, saying, "He think he could take who? That boy couldn't take a shit." They were so completely distinguished and different, so entirely themselves, it warmed me to watch them—they almost stood a chance. They offered two complete worlds to the marriage, two worlds in opposition, the pressures of which the marriage would have to stand against and be made stronger. When two white people married, God help them. Unless they had some deep division of class to bless them, some irreconcilable political difference to light their way, what was there to toughen them, to strengthen their bond together, but their own selves? And when was that ever enough?

I felt so kind toward them that day. Calyph got off the phone and sat back down, and again the serval ran off, and Antonia went on snipping, snipping, and he picked up one of her cuttings and turned it like he didn't know where the up of it was, and then set it down again and sighed, and his head sank as though he were resuming the pace of this world. After a moment her hand came quietly out, and ran down his arm, and cupped the elbow. It was a privilege just to watch them, really. It filled me with a funny feeling, a healthy jealousy, so warm and peculiar it was like the beginnings of love itself. The strength of their smallest gestures filled me with hot liquid light. I didn't want to break them up at all—I just wanted to sit there and take notes. In that moment I really did want only the best for them.

And then he began to kiss her. He leaned down over her, their faces were obscured. And why should he not? Well and good, I told myself. Let him have her. I bent to my work, my hand firm on the paper.

"You know he's watching us," she said.

It must have been the sudden noise in the quiet, but my hand jumped then. I'd been writing out the details of the best cars and in the midst of "tape deck" I made a deep slash across the paper. The page was ruined—I'd have to begin again.

"I'll go out back," I said quickly, very nonchalant and businesslike, but even as I stood I could feel myself seethe. I'd not been watching them, or not when she said I had—and not ever in that way she meant. And all at once it was too much for me. I felt almost spat upon, like she'd walked over and called me a peeping little lackey. I felt the affectionate jealousy cool and harden into something other, and, whistling, telling myself I was brushing it off, that I still felt happy, I went out to the car. It was misting, and when I went in the glove box for the house flyer, with the Realtor's little handscrawled note in the corner—"Great to meet you, Antonia!"—I put the thing carefully in my pocket, so the ink would not get damp.

When I stepped back into the kitchen, the serval came running. "First alert," I heard Calyph cry, and then the thing was circling my legs, chirping. I knelt down and knuckled it beneath its chin and along the sides of its face as the streaks of scent faintly wet my knuckles. I looked into its eyes to see if it saw trouble; it stared back at me blankly. I folded up the flyer and slipped it into one of his pricing guides, protruding like a fat bookmark.

When I crossed to go out back, I saw he had her in his arms. They were dancing. I stopped in the doorway, and I could not look away. She reached both her hands up to his face and ran her thin, splintered-looking fingers through his beard. Then she reached up again and pulled on his ears to make him bend down, her face flushing with the quick, childish assertion of need. It was adorable, and bending down he was so swelled with pride and calm he looked bored, as a lion looks bored. I watched their lips meet once more.

Swaying to the song's tender mope, she drew away, and their dance became goofy, and entirely unselfconscious, and when they began to kick up their feet and shimmy at one another, I knew I'd been forgotten. I didn't know whether to break something minor so they would look at me, or grit my teeth and try to forgive them, or just to go away, and then Calyph pivoted, as if to give a specially strong kick, and his knee gave way beneath him, and as he crumpled to the ground I heard a little pop, as if a jar had been unsealed.

(4)

The next morning was cloudless again. In a breeze sweet with the smell of pines baking in the sun, I took my laptop to the window, found an unsecured connection, and looked across the Internet for Calyph. I found him on the ESPN sidebar, with the secondary news:

WEST TO UNDERGO MICROFRACTURE SURGERY, MISS SEASON

Portland, Ore.

Less than a week after agreeing to a five-year, $32 million contract extension, the Portland Trail Blazers announced that forward Calyph West will undergo microfracture surgery on his left knee, and is expected to miss all of the upcoming season.

West, the 14th overall pick in the 2004 draft out of North Carolina, was expected to compete with Travis Outlaw for a starting spot at the small forward position. Last year he averaged 10.7 points and 3.9 rebounds in 21.5 minutes a game.

"Calyph's been a great addition over the past three years," Blazers general manager Kevin Pritchard said. "Obviously, we believe he's a core part of our team, and fortunately we think he's young enough to make a full recovery. In the meantime, we do feel we have great depth at the position."

West is scheduled to fly to Birmingham, Ala., where the surgery will be performed by Dr. James Andrews. He is expected to be on crutches for up to eight weeks. Full recovery likely will take six to 12 months, the team said. The Trail Blazers would not comment on the status of West's new contract.

It was a distant, ignorant thing, and I wanted to pour more life into it. Never having been close to an event worthy of the sporting news, it'd never occurred to me that every dry summary must be backed by a weight of intimate and unprintable detail, the meows and dances of a private life. I was there, I wanted to shout, I know about it all. But what was Calyph to them? The next year would be the worst of his life, his career could be in jeopardy, and yet all the people open to that page at the same moment as I, what did they feel? A distant satisfaction. They had gone hoping for news and there was some. The world was going round. Even if they were fans, they'd say, "Well, that clears up the rotation."

It was hard to know whether to feel responsible. I went back and forth about the sculpture a thousand times. He'd seemed fine afterward, had worked himself out and been satisfied. Still, I remember the look on his face when he leapt away from the ice. With knees sometimes it's the smallest thing.

After we heard the pop, he lay there a moment, looking only perplexed, like he'd tried to sit in a broken chair. I could see Antonia's face go gaunt with uncertainty, frozen in the last moment when denial was still possible. He clutched his knee with both hands, slowly, not like it pained him but like he wanted to gather it up and put it back together. Then he whimpered, once, a reedy, terrible sound, so distant from his ordinary voice it was like a note from a flute. He shook his head fiercely.

"I'm hurt," he said. "I'm hurt." And then she was on her knees.

The cat, sensing fun, bounded over and began to frolic. Antonia pushed it away, which only made it more rambunctious. Calyph shouted for me and I came out of the doorway and tried to grab the thing. I whiffed and it leapt away, chirping ecstatically, then rounded on me, waiting gamely for me to fail again. It led me from room to room, hunched over and mortified, locked in perverse and overmatched contest. The beast was spouting a sort of joyous horking sound. I remember thinking they must be able to see me hunching from room to room, the sounds of my hushed and desperate coaxing an absurd backdrop to their misery. At last I got the thing cornered in the kitchen and took it in my arms. I could barely keep from hurling it into the sink and running the disposal, just to see if a bit of limb might get nicked off. With the thing pinned writhing to my chest, I took back the house flyer and slipped it in my pocket. I guess I felt I'd done enough.

"Hush now," I heard him say behind me, as I went up the stairs to lock the cat in. "It'll be all right. Get the phone."

When I got the serval in a bedroom, it was bouncing and chirping all over. I looked around to see if the thing had a bed somewhere, like that would calm it, but all its things were in some other room. I tried the closet, and when I opened it the cat darted right in and plunged its front paws into a laundry basket, its hind still protruding into the room. It seemed occupied with snuffling the whites, so I made a move for the door. The next I knew the serval was busting past me into the hall, free again and horking joyously, a pair of Antonia's dirty silks dangling around its neck. It ran round and round the upper floor, sounding its triumph. I was looking for something to club it with when it ran back into the bedroom of its own accord. I locked it in the closet, and when I got back downstairs Calyph had his T-shirt pulled over his face. They told me to go right home and talk to no one.

He must have been on his way to Alabama already, but no one had called me. Someone else must have driven him to the airport. Throughout the night, while I slept, forces had been moving, and by dawn the panic was gone and agents of supreme competence had converged to handle everything. Hours before my first yawn of the morning I'd been cut from the loop and replaced.

When afternoon came and there was no word, I called the house line and his brother Talib answered.

"This is Jess," I said.

"Who?"

"The driver."

"Oh. Just, uh, sit tight. We'll let you know when he get back."

"Is everyone else there with him?"

"Where with him," he said curtly.

"Birmingham. It's in all the news."

"What do the news know?" he said, his voice aggressive with the strain of keeping up the cover.

"I just want to know if I'll be needed. How long does the surgery take?"

"Surgery?" he repeated incredulously.

"I was *there*."

He sighed. "Listen, people been callin'. Wantin' to know. I don't know who's who—I'm just tryin' to hold it down here. I wouldn't expect anybody back for three, four days at least. All right?" Then he hung up.

I tried to think of the time off as a luxury, but there was little to do. Some cloths I'd ordered for the car came in the mail and I touched the fine, soft fibers sadly. Once more I moved listless through the downtown streets, walking past the old happy-hour bars that had been nightly destinations in my past life as an ordinary Portlander, with a job at a nonprofit and a social life beyond my place of employment. I'd hardly been back from Northern a week when I realized all that was gone, that the whole scene I'd known had moved on, to marriage or to new discontentments I had no place in, or to California. My return to this city of youth, this city I'd once moved eighteen hundred miles to on the basis of a simple Web survey at FindYourSpot.com, had made me a stranger again. On my third morning off, I got a text that said "home soon," and I was glad.

Antonia's absence had made me feel the leanness of my life, and that night I bought a magnum of Belgian tripel, to remind myself of my proximity to eminence. As I drank I wandered through the bachelor's rooms, looking for treasures. I found a collection of foreign hotel soaps, a couple of bottles of white rum with faded Spanish labels, and, lying in a corner amid some camping gear, an old hickory switch, as smooth as if it had been oiled. A closet I'd never inspected before went back and back, and I took a flashlight in, expecting a grow room. Instead I just found the light switch, and, in an immaculate corner, a small lamp that lit up a tiny shrine to the bachelor's departed cat. The shrine had a Buddhist air, but its centerpiece was a Polaroid of the old tabby crouching proudly behind a dead bat. The cat was obese, and it was hard to believe the thing had come across a bat pitiful enough to be killed by it. It looked a little puzzled at its own prowess, crouching there in a crooked shadow that must have belonged to the bachelor himself.

As I reached down to flip the Polaroid over, my phone chimed back in the kitchen. "Late nite pickup?" it said, and I drank my glass down and watched the foam lace my empty chalice. For a moment in the garage I considered my sobriety, but as Calyph once assured me, only black men got pulled over in Jaguars.

Twenty minutes later I hit the chalk in Dunthorpe, and there under the floodlights Antonia stood on her steps, shivering in a party dress. She got her own door before I could, and I could see the gooseflesh coming down her shoulder.

"Why didn't you wait inside?"

"I wanted to wake myself up." She spoke fast, and her breath seemed short from the chill. "I walked around the house. You ever walk around outside your own house at night? And look up at the walls, and there's so much out there you never really looked at? It's like how could it be your house really, until you knew about it all?"

"No," I said. "Never."

"There's all this wood out there," she said. "There's all this stone. Come and look."

I looked at her there, dolled up, lined around the eyes like I'd never seen her, shivering through some unknowable mood. A woman puts on eyeliner and suddenly she's nocturnal and difficult. She looks like she could be a fatal problem. "The climate's controlled in here," I said.

"Come and look," she said again. "It's the wilderness out there."

I left the car running and let myself be led upon the lawn, around the side of the house, to where the chimney rose up. It didn't seem remarkable. They just looked like some white-bread quarry rocks to me. She strode toward the chimney and put her little slipper-shoe up on one of the stones of the corner and hoisted herself. I remember her little knee flashing, and the unexpected freckles of her leg as it bent in the moon.

She stepped into a little hop and slapped a rock at the apex of her jump, damn near seven feet in the air. "I own you," she cried at the rock as she hit it.

She landed in a crouch and still her eyes were on the chimney's tower of moon-white stone. "I own that," she said, in a puzzled voice.

When we came back to the car, I saw movement in the dark. Looking back at the house I saw the front door ajar, and a thin figure standing shrouded in the aperture. She stepped forward and I saw a woman with her arms crossed. She too was dressed and made up as if for a night on the town. Her face gleamed down on us petulantly, and I could see a tattoo on her calf.

Antonia must have followed my gaze, because she stopped in the drive. "What?" she asked the girl harshly. "What do you want? There's nothing to say."

Some kind of complicated rebuke passed over the girl's face, and she took another step toward the car. Antonia motioned abruptly for me to get her door, as if to forestall her. "Don't wait up," she said, and the girl melted back into the dark.

Out on the road we blew the heat and I edged around Antonia's wild mood.

"She was at the party," I began, but Antonia waved her hand disgustedly through the air.

"Anything but her," she said.

"Okay. How is he?"

"He's well enough—there wasn't anything for me to do. The family's all there."

"I didn't expect you so soon."

"It's not that long of a surgery, really. For what it is. For where they break your knee on purpose."

"Is he definitely out for the year?"

"He is. I think they're still going to pay him, though."

She said it like she actually thought that was what mattered to him. I glanced over, and the look of her dark painted eyes pained me. I wished she hadn't done that to herself. It made all the strange wildness, which otherwise might seem like a reckless opening of herself I was privileged to see, into trouble. I had a premonition that she was gathering all the trouble we could ever have into this night and loosing it, to have it out and behind her.

"Where are we going?" I asked. I'd just been driving toward everything not in her house that we could care about at that hour.

"Let's go to a strip club," she said instantly.

"Excuse me?"

"I am a girl who just wants to have fun," she said in a strange, wry voice, as if quoting someone else's assessment of her.

Clubs were not a totally foreign subject between us. The first time I'd ever been to a strip club had been delivering food, and she'd once trapped me in a painfully elaborate story about bringing Cobb salads to cabarets and lingerie modeling houses. She liked to tease me about going to this one place, Sassy's—I think she thought I had a habit. But I didn't want to go to a club. They were the only places in the city where I found it impossible to desire anything. I tried to imagine what kind of man it was who could get pleasure from laying dollar bills in front of a naked girl. Who could make a healthy, honest transaction out of that? I tried to imagine what type of man it took, what his face would look like, as he lorded over his little table with his roll of bills, laughing to his friends, taking a girl's sass and throwing it back to her, comfortable, enlivened, and unwithered.

"Which one?" I asked.

"You know which," she said, and we flew on toward the rain-washed, incalculable city.

As we came over the bridge, I decided I'd just drive on. So many times I'd been poised at the edge of something like this, a real break. I'd just drive on, past the club and into the teeth of the night, and wait for my nerves to tell me what I should do.

"Can I make a rule?" I asked.

"What?"

"No texting in the club. I don't want you there just passing the time. If you're in, you're in."

She laughed. "All right."

"Why don't I hold on to it."

"You're confiscating me?"

"That's right."

"I can just turn it off."

I held out my hand and she gave it over with a big sigh. As I brought the phone down into the door cavity, I bounced it off the child locks to set them.

Turning off Grand, an Escalade pulled up alongside us at the light. It was the universal model, black with chrome rims of restrained ostentation. I didn't recognize the car from the players' garage, but in our whitewashed city every driver of an Escalade seems a baller, and I tried to make out who was inside through the tint.

The car stayed with us to the red on Seventh, and then the passenger door popped for a second and someone spat out onto the roadbed. I got a glimpse of tan work boots. Until then, it might have just been some housewife on an ice cream run. I had a sudden sure feeling of where they were headed. Though they'd cleaned up their public image, the team still went to the club. It was the lifestyle league wide, you couldn't buck it any more than you could drive a Camry or work at an electronics store in the off-season. "Only people don't go to the club are the serious Christians and Doug Christie types," Calyph had said once. "And me, if A ask you."

I tried to think of who might be driving. Oden could only be in the backseat, slouched, unsure, coming along for the camaraderie. Roy was too much the face of the team, sitting his firstborn on his lap during press conferences. He could be shotgun. They could be his tan boots, so bright and clean they could move through any room without taint. It was probably some modest old veteran leading the expedition. Maybe it was just Steve Blake, skinny and white as me. I wondered what Antonia would do, seeing someone who knew her. We'd have to duck out or join them.

I supposed they'd be the sort to know how to carry them-selves. I could see their faces, sure and easy, demonstrating how to be supreme club clientele. I could see them being offered a private room, and waving it off—it wasn't that kind of night. They would turn away the Cristal and the status cognac and order all manner of odd drinks, and I could see us among them, in a palatable sort of experience. There might even be a brother-hood to it, as with Calyph on those rare times. "You don't need to tip fives," I saw Greg saying, like a guy in an instructional video that helps the beginners. "Just be consistent!"

"It's there on the left," she said, as we went by the club. I'd slowed a little, but only just. I saw the road in front of us, empty and wide, and then I saw the Escalade turn into the club lot behind us.

"Yes, ma'am," I said, and let the life of wild possibilities leak away yet again, and turned to park in the tree-shaded dark.

By the time we got in line, whoever was in the Cadillac was already inside. Antonia had brought a thin hoodie and slipped it over her shoulders. As soon as she had it on, she put up a tough face to go with it. It wasn't such a bad look—with her gleaming knees and the thin crepe of her dress's fringe beneath, she looked like one of those mythical halfsy-halfsy creatures. I wished I could pull her hood up, so the image would be complete.

When we got to the bouncer, the atmosphere of the place came at us in its smoke and din. These were the years before the smok-ing ban, and the air was so thick it was like a community effort. The only element of the place not stained by smoke was the liquor itself, and everyone was diving down after that purity. I watched the bouncer run a thick finger around inside Antonia's tiny bag.

I saw her to a table and excused myself—for the bathroom,

I said. I headed for the back stage, hoping to see familiar figures towering over the rail, their jewelry aglitz in the black light. Coming around the corner I could see there wasn't any flash like that. The stage was empty, and beneath it I saw a guy in a leather jacket and tan boots at a table with his friends. Something had gone wrong with them. I could see the dull skin of their crewcut scalps. Their heads were square and null as new erasers. I watched them shining the dull, unforgivable shine of my own people. I turned away with the bitterest feeling.

At our little table, beneath a plastic banner that proclaimed "It's the Water," Antonia was pushing up her sleeves and letting down her zipper. Two pints had appeared. I went through the smoke, past the hungry faces of men pretending to be fed. The club was full and disordered, and I had to pass near the stage to get by. A dancer smiled a terrible smile. Her nipples were hard, like objects all their own. Of course I felt naked.

I got to my seat and Antonia took a long drink from her pint. It looked any color but gold.

"I'm driving, you know," I said.

"This is NA beer."

On the near stage, a girl with purple hair had focused her energies on a man at the rail. His face was young but his hair was prematurely gray. It was the first dance, she was still clothed, but she was locked in, staring down at him with electric contempt. She slapped herself on the thighs, the sounds puncturing the music. She squeezed her breasts together like she wanted to mistreat them. The man was cringing and bent and dropping bills over the rail all the time.

"I'll get some cash," I said.

She pulled out a wad of singles and patted it. "I'm paying for this," she said.

"Madame appears seasoned."

She shrugged a little, and you could see she was proud. "I used to go in college. Just me and the ladies."

I lifted my pint. "To temperance," I said.

"To an understanding." I took a sip of the beer, and it was pretty well Pabst, and I knew I had no understanding of anything. Of course, there was a certain line of thought—the girl in the door, whoever she was and whatever they'd had, and then this, Antonia watching, relaxed and intent, as the first dance ended and the tops came off. The girl with purple hair slung herself out there indifferently. But in tracing this line, I felt the leap of it, the stupid male paranoia it required, the belief that a woman's unhappiness was an abandonment waiting to happen, that always, at any moment, we could be betrayed in favor of anyone of either gender.

"So, is this your last bit of fun?" I asked.

She laughed. "I hope not. Is it yours?"

"Not yet."

She took a long but somehow elegant drink, like a thirsty person in a commercial. "I suppose I am," she said, "rededicating myself."

"You like men after all," I said helpfully.

She looked at me with pity.

"And women, too, of course. But. Except . . ."

When she spoke it was like she only wanted to stop my floundering.

"I was going to leave him," she said, in a plain, clear voice. "And now I'm not." When she said it she was even looking at the dancers, not casually, but as though they absorbed her as much as anything.

"Oh," I said.

"Yes. That house? Forget that house. I don't want it. I'm letting it fall through." She took another long drink. "Do you like them to be real?" she asked abruptly.

"What?"

Only then did she look at me, and the look was direct, almost severe in its scrutiny. "On your dancer. Do you like them to be real, or not?"

"Yes," I said. "Real."

"Really? I like the fakes," she said. "If she were my wife I'd want them to be real. Otherwise, so what."

I looked over at her, at the tough cross of her arms and the jaunty angle of her head. Her hardened poses sat oddly atop her real blend of sensitivity and indifference. When I was hardly less than her age and delivering my food, I truly did not want to look. It was almost a pleasure to deny myself, to ensure that the body of the woman I might have been about to meet would never be lessened by overfamiliarity.

"The fakes used to scare me, I remember," she went on. "Like I was looking at these bags. There were four of us, we were just nineteen. Me and Sally and Ginger and . . ." Her voice fumbled a moment. "I don't know if we liked it. The men our parents might've known eating steak. The thought that they'd come over, napkins tucked into their collars, and try to talk to us. But it felt daring. I thought, I'm going to be a new woman, this is the first step."

As she talked I saw the pose slip, and the callousness I could never quite believe in replaced by the look of someone lit from within, reliving something, as if a new wind were blowing across her eyes the old yellow-cornered pictures of gone seasons.

On the near stage, the purple was preparing for her last dance. A bonanza of dollars lay scattered on the rail in front of the gray-haired man. His face was cracked into a parched smile.

"You want this?" she said, slamming her heel on the rail. I

imagined my fingers twisting beneath. "You want this?" she shouted over the music. Under the rail's shelf I could see one of his legs, shaking uncontrollably.

She circled the stage until the pole was between her and the man. Grabbing it underhand, she turned away and set her terrifying shoes in place. She pulled herself backward into the pole with a violent collision, as if the pole was having its way with her from behind. She did it again and the pole shook.

"Like this?" she cried, slamming herself backward. "Baby? Where are you, baby? Talk to me when you fuck me. Why are you so quiet?" There was some laughter, and I thought how common something had to be, to bring this crowd together. We were all so happy it wasn't us, this shaking man, that it wasn't our eyes that watched the ceiling of the stage as the pole shook, knowing in a second it would cave in on us for all we had come here to want.

Antonia looked delighted.

"But why would you leave him?" I asked finally. I felt weakened by bringing him up; it made me feel my subservience. But I saw his stern face and his crumpled legs, as though they were projected into the smoke-thick air, pressing down over us.

"I won't," she said.

"Now that he's injured you can't," I said softly.

"No," she said. "But that's not why."

"He won't be down forever."

"We'll be different people when he's well. We'll have come through something. And I want to. I want to nurse him. I'm going to order the best sheets. Fifteen-hundred-thread-count Egyptian cotton. In the mornings we'll lie there and eat omelets and watch documentaries. At night I'll sleep in a cot by his side. I'll never leave the house. I'll be his wife and nurse him. I want to nurse him until it seals us off and makes another world."

As she said it, I could see their future together—warmer,

wiser, less young. The glamour would have fallen off them a little, but they'd be the better for it, more knit-up. There was no place for me in that world. They might as well be driven by a mute fugee in a cream suit.

"Don't you see?" she asked. "You can't tell him. Won't you keep that house and all between us?"

I gave her a shrug. "What can you offer?"

She brushed her hair back from her face with a slow finger, looking away, like it was a task that took the greatest care. "You're a funny one."

"You'd probably do anything," I said. "Anything I asked."

"I won't," she said quickly. "But there's a lot you'd never think to ask for."

Before I could think of asking what, she ran her hand abruptly through the poisoned air, forestalling me, gesturing at every-thing. Suddenly I could think of nothing to say, nothing to push our talk further into the explicit.

"You'll have no need for me," I said instead. "Lying in bed all day."

"I'm sure we'll find something for you to do."

"I could take you to get your own car. I'll drive you to the DMV for your exam, and that'll be it."

"You know, I *do* have—"

"You'll want to buy some magazines before you go," I ex-plained to her. "You won't like the ones they have."

She laughed, but I could tell she didn't find it funny.

"Imagine the two of you," I said in a bright, friendly voice. "A player and his wife, living only for one another. What'll you do on road trips? Drive behind the bus, talking to him on the phone?"

"They fly everywhere," she said tightly.

"You make him sit in the back so you can look at him," I went on cheerfully. "You make him wave to you while the other players turn away. If a woman looks at him wrong you come after her in the stands. When he shoots free throws, he does a special little thing for you with his pinkie."

She turned away from me abruptly, and when her hand reached back for the pint it shook. She took a long drink, put the glass down, then spun back and hit me in the shoulder with her little fist.

"What?" I tried to laugh but it was just my mouth moving.

Again she punched me, with her little, lively, harmless-looking fist. I could feel a knot begin to draw together.

I tried to sound reasonable. "You brought me here to hit me?"

"I brought you because I thought you might be able to stop looking at *me*," she said.

I felt my vision go wider. It was like I could see all the stages at once now, all the girls with their terrible smiles in the heady and wasting neon air.

"Come on, hit me back," she said.

"This NA is getting you drunk."

"Hit me," she taunted. "It's the closest you'll get."

I turned and looked at the sign over the bar, which listed about forty-six things you couldn't do inside the club. I'd been going through it before, while the gray-haired man broke down at the rail.

"It says no punching women," I said, pointing vaguely.

As I turned back I felt her on my ear. I felt her short nails bite as she twisted the lobe.

I heard a strange sound then. I thought I heard a man far off, beyond the lacquered walls, keening in a high, effeminate voice. I saw my arm twisting back, moving hers aside and reaching out, gripping the strings of the hood, pulling her toward me. It shouldn't have worked, but she came forward willingly, almost softly, as if compelled. She had a fearful, rapt, knowing expression on her face, as if I were doing something fated she'd long waited for.

I felt my mouth soften and my eyes go half-closed. I imagined my face as someone else's, a soft, sensitive face with a curling, brutal mouth. I let the strings go loose in my hand, but still I held them.

"We'll go now," I said. My voice had gone deeper.

She nodded, suddenly obedient and demure. "I only thought you'd want to look at these girls."

"It's no substitute," I said. "Put your hood up."

"What?"

I reached across and lifted the hood and put it over her head softly. For a moment she looked like a mysterious androgyne. She didn't protest. "Pay the dancer," I said, and she went and shyly laid the bills onto the rail. The dancer was collecting her clothes; she looked at Antonia curiously.

I went out into the alley. I felt myself shaking, exultant and terrified that she'd obeyed. Expressionless under the low clouds, I stood and waited one minute, and then two, and then she came out, still wearing the hood, and I opened the door for her, and closed it tenderly behind, and we rode through the red-lit city, with all the buildings as distant and unchanging as if they had been captured inside a glacier of perfect ice. Through silent canyons we rode home to the bachelor's house.

Bringing her round at last, I did feel proud. The carriage house where I garaged the car looked antique and strange in the dim cloud-light; the old house itself seemed to stand timeless and tall as some ancestral home. I'd used the place once or twice, to fill in some detail about my fallen family, so to come on it now was a sort of homecoming. Its disintegrations were soaked with night, half-invisible. Even the landlady's house cat, who had previously proven himself to be a simple machine that turned kibble into yowling, managed to be picturesquely asleep beneath the grandfather clock in the foyer. The second floor was dark, and I took Antonia's hand easily and led her up to the attic stair.

For all I'd thought of having her there, I can't say I was prepared. As I turned the knob, the next image my mind offered was of her lying facedown over the edge of the bed. But I didn't want to go right to that. I wanted to show her some class, and make her feel at home. As we got up on the landing I even had a strange feeling of satisfaction already, as if having her for my guest was all I'd wanted.

I made us some drinks, with pineapple juice and the bachelor's rum, like we were just a couple of old friends kicking it there in that Mardi Gras mausoleum. I handed her the cool glass and we went from room to room, turning on all the lights, and the old beads and relics of revelry shone dully, projecting their weathered best in perpetual sad festival. There was a poignancy in having Antonia look at these things, as though the bachelor's old walls were gazing at her with reverence and crying out yes. I took up the glasses and we went and looked at his books of love.

"*Loving a Woman in Two Worlds*," she read, marveling. As soon as I failed to assault her she'd grown calm again.

I showed her *Sacramental Acts* and *If the Buddha Dated*, and while I wanted her to be amazed by this accumulation of overly heartfelt advice, this embarrassment of embarrassment, I was glad she didn't laugh. I wanted her only to be in awe, as if observing the ritual of some strange and derided religion.

Next came the cat shrine. I clicked on the small lamp with the Bourbon Street shade that gave the corner its own rich light, and she knelt on the carpet amid the mothballs and picked up the old Polaroid by its corners.

She flipped it over. "Sabonis," she read. "Your name was Sabonis."

She sat back, thinking.

"Be right back. Is that okay?" She waited for me to nod and then her bare leg brushed by me in the narrow way. I heard the door to the apartment creak open.

I looked at her little handbag, tipped beneath the mustard suits. I thought of opening it, but I was a little afraid there would be nothing in there. I imagined digging through some lip balms looking for an object that reassured me there was some strangeness worth seeking within her cultivated origins and the bright flits of her little heart, and how I would feel if it weren't there. Instead I hopped to, and collected a few of the things I'd need for later. I found the hickory switch and slid it under the bachelor's old four-poster.

When Antonia came back to the closet, she had a handful of books and the house cat in her arms. He wriggled out and fell heavily to the floor, glaring around with a haughty look.

"This is for you," she said, handing me what looked like a comic pamphlet.

"'El Libro Del Amor, numero 511,'" I read.

For herself she showed a volume by the Kensington Ladies' Erotica Society.

"You're reading all these, right?" she asked, sipping the rum.

"Of course."

"By the time you get your own place, you'll know everything about love," she said. "You're so lucky."

I nodded gravely, and we turned to our books. The cat padded shyly over to her, and she showed him the cover and underlined the title with her finger for his benefit. He snuffled her knees, then climbed carefully into the hollow of her crossed legs and plumped down.

"'Denuded, he was as stark and white as the cliffs of Dover, and just as hard,'" Antonia read. "'His reverent face gleamed up at mine and I partook at last of the soft stone of his unscabbarded delicacy.'"

We laughed, and I wondered if I ought to feel emasculated, smiling so benignly at this girl over whom I'd just been asserting my command. It was a sort of relief to let that slip away a bit, to just be two people again, with no pressure on us. Still, I knew if I just let her off altogether she wouldn't respect me.

"What have you got there?" she asked.

I'd taken some spare sheets from a little blue cabinet the bachelor kept, and I was twisting them up and tying loose knots in the ends.

"What are those for?"

"You know," I said. She'd put her head in, so she'd have seen the four-poster.

"Let me help," she said, and reaching her slow hand out I let her take a corner. I watched her little fingers work quietly upon the soft blue sheets.

"Did you know," she said finally, "I married him because I thought he'd cheat."

She brushed her finger over the soft, folded ear of the sleeping cat distractedly.

"I thought we'd be young and in a new city and he'd be famous and it'd be kind of dazzling like that for a while, and then it'd settle down and he'd cheat and then I could do what I wanted again."

The cat flicked its ears and began to purr through its nose in a lively snort.

"Only he didn't," she finished. "And then I didn't know what to do." She looked down at the cat beseechingly.

She was sitting at the edge of the light, so her face and hands were warm and whiskey-colored, lit up with all the rich life that the bachelor yearned for us, his guests, to know that he had known, while the back of her neck looked only meager by the closet's bare bulb. I saw her there, leaning into the light, and again I thought I understood something of her want. She seemed to want only life. I saw her at home in Dunthorpe, with Calyph gone to Cleveland or Charlotte to play eighteen minutes a game and then not hit the town, pacing restlessly in a house she must have still been trying to own. I imagined she'd walk out at night onto one of several balconies and look up the riverbank at the distant city lights as though they were shining on some inaccessible nocturne society, that she had neither the transportation to nor the language for. Just to have been up here, and not there, must have felt like all the difference.

Our glasses were empty, and when I came back she was lying with her face toward the wall. The dress had ridden up a little, and the skin above her knees looked like she'd bathed in milk her whole life.

"Whenever you're ready," she said, her face to the wall. Her voice was dead and indifferent but she almost gasped at the end, she had so little breath. I took up the sheets and the old, soft shirt that I thought would serve as a blindfold. It had the lineup from a jazz festival on it, and I hoped when we were done she might like to sleep in it, it was so soft and worn.

In the bedroom I put my glass on the table and fixed the sheets to the posts of the bed. They were light blue with little sunflowers. All in all, I thought it was a soothing setup. It would be just like tying up your wife.

When I turned to fetch her she was already standing in the door, watching me. Her face was tight again, but I thought I saw a curiosity there. It was like when she'd given me that chiding look, for kissing her, but beneath you could see she was pleased. She frowned as if she found the setup distasteful, but that just made me wonder if she'd done it before.

"I'll let you do your legs yourself," I said. There was an armchair just past the foot of the bed, where the sun fell in the afternoons, and I sat back to watch, stirring the new ice of my drink.

Slowly she took her shoes off and slipped the knots around her ankles. She stared me down as she yanked each tight.

"Take off that hood," I said. "You'll want to loosen your dress."

She stared at me strangely, proud, unwilling to divulge herself. At last she threw the hoodie aside and I got up and did her arms. The skin of her wrists was like damp paper faintly inked. I bound her very gently; I wanted her to have some play. Last I prepared the old shirt for the blindfold.

"Is that necessary?"

"I thought we had an understanding," I said. I expected her to scoff, but she just closed her eyes dutifully, waiting for the cloth. I could hardly believe it myself, that she was so acquiescent. It couldn't have been just to get me to be silent. She told herself that was all it was, a trial to be undergone to achieve some end, all the while wanting it. She must have been having her own daydreams for years. I wound the old shirt around her gently. Then I stood at the foot of the bed, savoring it a moment, rising up to my fullest height though there was no one to see.

"Please take off your dress," I said.

She lifted all four of her limbs at once, in helplessness, like a flipped turtle. I suppose she meant to be funny.

"It should come with a little work," I assured her.

I saw her face twist in genuine confusion beneath the wrap of cloth. "Did you forget which part was supposed to come first?"

I reached beneath the bed then, and brought up the switch.

It was the thinnest thing, a toy really, but she didn't know that. I sent it whistling down onto the bed beside her, where it made a good crack.

"I didn't forget," I said.

"What's that?" she asked quick.

"I won't have to use it, I'm sure," I said with great confidence. I sent it down on the other side of her, just for symmetry, and she set to work.

The straps of her dress weren't much trouble. They were thick, but she could just bite them and work them off the shoulder. She shrugged her shoulders in circles and a bit more of her appeared, though nothing that was new to me. But then she had to get creative. She tried dragging herself along the bed, but it wasn't any help. She'd have to really exert herself, to wriggle even, to make any progress. She didn't want to do that, I could tell. She forgot she was a willing prisoner and wanted to be a dignified one.

"I give up," she said. "Come help me."

But she'd hardly tried. So I switched her, just once, very gently with the tip of the thing. She gasped, and for a moment she seemed very fragile, like she might cry, but then she went hard and still again, her teeth bared.

"You should have loosed it properly," I said.

"Do you see a zipper?" she asked, full of disdain. Of course she was right. It just came off over her head; it didn't loosen at all.

"You'll just have to try very hard," I said. I sent the switch down a lot then. It was only on the bed of course, but it was all around her, she could hear it whistling through the air, it was a bit psychological. She began to really struggle at last. Beyond caring how she looked, she twisted and writhed upon the bed. At last the tips of her soft debutante's breasts slid out into the light.

She felt her exposure and sank back. She was breathing heavy. Even this small nudity shocked me, her nipples were so dark. There was a bright red line on her calf where I'd switched her.

The moment pressed upon me. Again I felt unprepared. I'd only gotten the sheets so the night would seem to have a direction. Once she'd seen me prepare them, I had to use them. I only wanted to have control.

But then, I reminded myself, she'd been having these dreams, too, about servants, all her girlhood probably. For every boy in a nowhere town taking the family car to the lake to see the distant figures on the private docks, there is a girl in a high window on a humid southern cul-de-sac, looking at the gardener. I was the gardener now, I reminded myself. She'd waited a long time for this, too. She'd tried to get it in marriage, but he would've transcended that by now. He couldn't be everything at once. Though he still loomed over all her life, he had lost his power, through the inarticulable diminishment of marriage. She wanted a substitute, some new body on its instinctual rise from obscurity, a self-made man still in the making.

Well, I would serve, I would serve.

I reached down and gripped her ankle, and put my mouth to her calf. I took off my belt so she could hear it whipping in the air.

Then from somewhere the cat jumped on the bed. The fat bulk of him must have had to go all out to reach such heights. Disregarding the petty human activities before him, he stalked around Antonia. Glaring at me, he slumped down along her hip. I showed him the switch and he looked ready to bat at it, and I reached to throw him down. But then Antonia laughed. All the tension of her surrender was released in a loud snort. The cat was backing its rump up into her side.

The whole feeling of the moment was changed somehow.

Suddenly I couldn't imagine moving the cat to get at her. The presence of this dumpy living thing, pathetically wholesome, the hairs of its belly disarrayed, asserted something that had been lying in my mind since the afternoon, since my first day maybe. I looked at her a long time. She was so little and lithe, I imagined undoing the bonds so she could pounce at me, the bachelor's sheets cheaply harsh next to her skin, and the rich fabric that would be by then hanging off her, torn.

I tried to imagine the vivid color of them as they sat on the floor, discarded in the wan morning light. I could see it, and I knew somehow it would be a disappointment. I'd get up and try to make her breakfast and remember I had no food, and feel that there was nowhere to go from there, that whatever else had pulled me to that job was beyond me now, and would go unexplored. And all for the pleasure of ripping a pair of underwear off the boss's wife, off a girl on whom I had hung a few of my more inexhaustible aspirations. It had seemed the rarest aim, the most illicit goal, but now it felt small to me. It had just been all I could think of to want.

I breathed softly, looking down at her, and I felt flush with sensitivity, delicate, mysterious to myself once more, and I knew that to force the rent underwear down her calves would only fill me with dread. To climb at last upon the bed would be to say, it's all been for this, I can make nothing greater.

It's not that I would have minded so badly. Of course I'd have had her, if there were no consequences. But what most obsessed me was elsewhere. I sensed again some other energy, that had called me to take this job, and that now made this great victory of sex and class—that she should say my name and not his while something within her was rending and I was pressing her face into a pillow—into a small man's triumph. I stood on the cusp; I felt it beneath my feet; I rocked forward and then settled back on my heels again, relieved. Her torn underwear and her cries would be some exquisite, stolen pleasure only in relation to whatever blank, middle-middle life had come before. As though I had ever had anything, really, to rise up from. What did I live by, to claim victory from that? What rich heart would feed on that and be full? No. There was more. There was Calyph.

"Just a second," I said, and I went out into the hall, to the kitchen. From among my work things I took up the Realtor's flyer, the one I'd planted and then taken back again after he'd been hurt. The little thing had seemed so dangerous once, and it was time to be rid of it. I picked it up and unfolded it with wide, disbelieving eyes. A picture of Joseph Jones stared back at me; his dapper staff stood handsomely arrayed. It was a leaflet for Lost Boys. I'd grabbed the wrong thing. I stood there a long time, thinking what it meant.

When I came back, she looked asleep. Softly I unbound her; her limbs sank down inert. The blindfold had slipped down, but still her eyes were closed. I smoothed the spread as I moved my hands away, and then her eyes were open and she was looking at me curiously, and I felt all through my limbs the pleasure of declining, the depthlessness of my own heart, and then a prickle of excitement, for whatever was in store for him and me, and then I turned away before I could get sorry, and walked from room to room, to turn out all the yearning lights and find somewhere to sleep.

PART
TWO

(5)

In the fall after the estrangement, I had him all to myself, crippled and more and more in need of me. The team had a lot invested in him, of course—there was always someone lurking, watching over his regimen. He had his mother and brother for the cooking and the housework. In interviews he'd give them credit for the emotional side of his recovery, for keeping him upbeat and on the right path. But really I think I did as much as anyone. What was he going to say? This white dude I hired to drive my car is really giving me a lot of support? They always credit their mothers, you can look anywhere.

Still, I was there. I was the one heating up the soup with the sandwiches his brother made three or four at a time and left to chill. I had so much business with crutches and pill bottles I was halfway an orderly. I even made his bed for him some days. The corners were so tight he couldn't tell it wasn't his mother. Late some nights, when he got tired of rolling toward another championship with his alma mater on the Xbox, we'd play Chinese poker, or just sit up talking. Sometimes he'd press me for details about my past, and it was almost embarrassing to see him devour tales of my grandmother, the famous Milwaukee socialite, and our family home on the bluffs over Lake Michigan. But he was a surprising listener for someone who'd been treated like junior royalty half his life, and it was hard to deflect his interest. He'd nod sagely at the description of the wrought-iron phaeton on our driveway gate, and these impossible details seemed to give him satisfaction, as though seeing our fall materialized reassured him of his own ascent.

It was hard to take more than a little pleasure from it, though. They were difficult times for him, and there was a grim feeling to everything. The days were full of gray light and rooms with drawn curtains. Still, I was happy. I'd worked my way into the center of things. I was dug in, I could watch and watch—and I was needed.

As for Antonia, I can't say I thought about her much. It was strange; she was gone so suddenly. I remember seeing her again for the first time a few days after I tied her to the bed, fleeting in the front doorway while I sat in the car, a fragment of a private smile hanging off her. Afterward she was always pushing her husband around in a wheelchair. But that phase didn't last, either—Calyph soon got well enough to find her out.

He found the flyer for her house on Alberta, which I could never manage to recover, in early August. He called the number and they told him everything. Then he just sent her away, and all for cheating on him with a little real estate. I thought for sure I'd be preoccupied a little, that she'd come to me in a daydream now and then. I guess when she didn't it seemed only respectful. He didn't desire her, so I didn't. She wasn't even illicit anymore, merely passé. I knew they weren't done with one another, not really, but he wanted to live in this illusion of complete erasure of her, and I complied. Through simple will he made a new, diminished world and walled her out of it, and then we lived there together, he and I, with his wounds.

In the middle of October, we went for a week to the Pharaoh's estate. Savier "Pharaoh" Ramses was the last of the Jail Blazers, the gifted but misbehaving old guard who had taken the team to the Western Conference finals in '99 and 2000 but bottomed out the franchise by the mid-aughts. Pharaoh had been a high draft pick during the team's decline, but he was one of those talents who never became more than a sideshow collection of impressively mismatched skills. He was six-nine with guard speed and a great handle, but had no half-court game: he was too weak for the post and he couldn't shoot. He was technically still with the team, but he'd not been on the active roster at all the previous season. The official reason was a slow-healing knee injury, but the rumor was that he and his bloated salary were getting pushed out. All summer I'd seen his classic Pontiac convertible with its "PH4R40" license plate haunting the players' garage. Ras, his Antiguan driver, liked to dispense paternal advice to me about car wax, and Pharaoh became a sort of mentor to Calyph, gifting him with the nickname Yoshi, or Young Sheed. The team probably would've given Calyph a bonus just for staying away from Ramses, but with their matching knee injuries and defiant on-court attitudes, there was no keeping them apart.

I arrived at the Pharaoh's as a guest, but soon found myself placed among the staff. I guess it was clear right away I wasn't going to be any good at smoking spliffs and sitting by the pool. "Come," said Ras, as I stood awkwardly in the doorway of my narrow room that first afternoon. "You'll see more of de place if you work a little. We'll only give you chitty-chitty stuff to do."

The gaming tent stood in the middle of the hanging gardens, which ran almost to the cliff in the southwest corner of the estate. The Pharaoh had built on a desolate stretch of coast about two hours from Portland, and at high tide I could hear the sea in all its violence. My week there was one of the most singular of my life, but few moments there thrilled me with as much consummate oddness as following Ras down a narrow stone path beneath dangling creepers, carrying gourmet BLTs on a blinding silver tray to men who sat in the hiss and boom of the seething Pacific, playing video games.

"Don't shoot that," came Calyph's voice. "That's not your range, boy."

"I hit that all day."

"Not on here you don't. They got you so you can barely make a damn layup."

"Naw," Belmont said, jockeying his controller around in unconscious compensation. "I show you." He wore a bright white T-shirt and a modest gold chain, and looked hardly more than a boy.

They crowded the wide set, and the low stools they sat on leaned dangerously as they traded fast breaks. Calyph's crutches sat against a nearby chair. Pharaoh lay behind them in a squat black chaise longue, watching indifferently. Only when we came beneath the tent did he grasp his cane to rise.

"Brick again," Calyph chided. "Better put Deron back in."

"Man, you musta put it to Superstar."

"I didn't put nothing to nothing, and you're oh for six from deep. You're playing this game like you twelve."

"I'm tellin' you, they got me rated *right*. Ninety-five speed."

"Yeah? Pause it, let's see. Let's see what rating they got for you from three."

"I'm like eighty," Belmont boasted. "Seventy-five, minimum."

"Let's see. Oh. Oh, sixty? Yeah. So sorry."

"What are you?"

"Doesn't matter," Calyph said quickly. "I never play as me. What am I, a damn egoist?"

"Food, gentlemen," Pharaoh called. "Pause that for now."

They rose quickly, and when Calyph hopped over to collect his crutches, he still managed a suggestion of grace. His leg was heavily braced, but the thing didn't look too medical—I'd helped him pick the color, a rich navy.

Pharaoh had three guests from the league that week, though none would be seen in any of the home openers that were by then less than two weeks away. Pharaoh and Calyph were injured, Belmont was suspended, and Goat, who was late, was just a failure.

Among the visiting servants, I was Calyph's only representative, while Belmont had a three-man entourage. In eighth grade, Rodrique Belmont had been a six-foot point guard from the Bronx with the best crossover since Washington did the Delaware, and now he was just a five-ten backup in Utah, a child prodigy seen through to a limited man. Hype died slow, and the league's contracts were guaranteed, so Belmont arrived with the trappings of the star he was once thought sure to become. Goat came alone, and I think he was already in debt.

As the men came near, I eyed the bacon and the wedges of avocado on the sandwiches hungrily, and watched Ras pour a clear, sparkling drink from a glass pitcher. Pharaoh, being a man of purity, forbade the presence of alcohol until sundown.

"To living in the league," he said, toasting in his rasping voice. "And to the player's freedom from enslavement—from the owner, from the coach, and from the dollar."

Calyph and Belmont glanced at each other a moment before lifting their glasses silently in the air, as if wary of the import of this stern rhetoric upon their weekend. Ras nudged me. A woman was coming down the path.

"Careful," he muttered. "You look at her, she talks to you."

As she was still much too far away to talk to me, this was a simple ploy. She was a short, white redhead, dressed in a gray tee cut ragged at the neck and sweatpants. She walked with her shoulders back, and I could see the sheen of sweat on her collarbones across the distance. Her body was just unfair, unfair to her I mean. I don't think she could play badminton, eat a strawberry, or even so much as read an advertisement for milk in a magazine without seeming to engage in a luscious and obscene activity. "She a hothouse flower in the champagne room," Calyph said later, and whatever that means, I can't say it better. As she grew near, a communal embarrassment seemed to come over everyone but the Pharaoh. She was the first woman we'd seen there who was not a servant, and Belmont hissed between his teeth as if in displeasure. I could see there was something strange with her hands.

As she came under the tent, Pharaoh put his hand on her shoulder just formally enough that I didn't draw any conclusions, and presented her as Odette. Her hair was up and her hands were wrapped in tape, like a fighter's. She wiped her arm across her brow and shook hands with poise, holding her left back gingerly.

"Did you hurt yourself?" Pharaoh asked.

"It's broken," she said, lisping. She held her small, battered hand up for us to see, but Pharaoh did not take her seriously, and everyone else seemed to think better of leaning in to look. After a moment she began to unwrap the tape proudly.

"Who were you fighting?" Calyph asked, looking away like he was amused.

"I was sparring with Wedge," she replied. "Do you know him?"

"He's a big man."

"He's always gentle with me," she said scornfully.

"Training for Ali, huh?" Belmont said. He too was looking away, expressionless, like something boring yet absorbing was happening over his shoulder.

"I don't really fight," she said. "But I need to train for my next set."

We took this cryptic remark without comment, and the slow soft ripping of the tape filled the air. I wondered if I'd seen her somewhere before.

"I need to shower," she said. "I only came down to steal a little food." Pharaoh motioned to the tray and she lifted a sandwich, then, sneaking her "broken" hand in coyly, took another.

"Puma," Pharaoh said sternly.

She put the second sandwich back sulkily and left the tent. No one watched her go.

That night Goat arrived a little before dark, and I saw him pull in from my basement window. His ride was unmistakable. It was a dark-purple Maybach with the conservative style of a European luxury line, but set so low to the ground on wheels so large that it bore a passing resemblance to the Batmobile. It was a princely car for a moody prince. The sense of uniqueness, or personality crisis, was heightened by the fact that the Maybach, not known for its efficiency, had been converted to biodiesel— its license read "BIO3." There was a dent in the rear fender that broke through the paint and didn't look recent.

Just three years ago, Lucas "Goat" Montaigne had been an All-American at Boise State, never much of a powerhouse. Goat didn't look like much of a player: he was a rail-thin wing, pale as a vampire, who came to fame wearing a black goatee with its mustache twirled. He was an incredible shooter and an emotional, almost hysterical player. He wept when he led Boise within a game of the Final Four, and once hurled a CBS camera off its stand after losing a rivalry game. All this made him a folk hero: the Larry Bird of the Northwest, or, as some magazine put it, The Great Emo Hope. When he declared for the draft, the Blazers were at their lowest and there was some local pressure to pick him in the top five to turn the franchise around.

Goat could score but he couldn't do much else. The Blazers passed on him and he played for two seasons in Milwaukee, where he was an epic bust. It's almost impossible for a rookie who's gone lottery to fall out of the league in less than four years, but Goat got exposed his rookie year and then he got injured. His contract was not extended, and when he was healed the Blazers brought him back to the city that had wanted him for its star on a ten-day free agent contract. He was just twenty-three.

I remember watching Goat's first game in Portland at a bar in Marquette, and when he was sent in with four minutes to go in a twenty-point loss, the crowd roared as it hadn't since the introduction of Oden. That roar was pure, the greeting of a savior, but the noise for Goat was louder, an outpouring of love for a neglected son whose failures were perhaps all attributable to the fact that we made him go and play in Milwaukee. We loved him guiltily and manically, even when we realized that his goatee was gone and his face looked sickly and ordinary. When he tore off his warm-ups in the fourth he looked stricken, a pariah edging back into society, and in four minutes he managed to miss three shots, turn the ball over twice, and get dunked on. In the final seconds, he caught a pass and swooped at the hoop as the defense sagged around him. As he got to the rim I had the inexplicable thought that if he blew the dunk, he would drown himself that night in the ocean. He didn't, but the buzzer rang too soon, and the shot didn't count.

Seeing he was alone, I stepped out and helped him with his bags. He was still clean-shaven and his hair was buzzed short for the court. After the almost Victorian poses of his popular years, this gave him the fragile look of a hospital patient newly released. He had a duffel and two sleek garment bags, both of which I managed to get from him after a little tussle of confusion. We didn't speak, and when Maxim met us at the door to take his luggage from me, Goat scrounged hastily in his pocket for a few dollars. It was a little endearing to deny him.

Because nothing could be drunk until sundown, everybody

stayed up late. On every night of the week but the last, the party retired around ten to the after-dinner room. It was designed something like a huntsman's lodge, which I say with all the certainty of never having been in one any more than Pharaoh had. There were dark beams crossing the ceiling, a chimney made of jagged stones, and a big fire. In one corner sat an unplugged arcade hunting game complete with plastic rifles. On the second night, I asked the Pharaoh if he hunted.

"Who am I, Colin Powell?"

I was about to banish myself to silence for the rest of the week when he shook his head a little wistfully and continued.

"I'd like to shoot a elk," he said. "Make me feel part of somethin'."

"Make you feel part 'publican," Belmont sang.

"Imagine that, doe," Pharaoh said, laughing huskily. "Half a dozen brothers go up to Montana, lookin' right, showin' dignity, shootin' at some elk. Why don't that happen?"

"Only baller who hunts is Karl Malone," Calyph declared.

"Nobody wanna be like Karl Malone," said Belmont, shaking his head with animation. "I mean, Utah *infect* a man. Who you know grew up in Louisiana, star baller, next thing you see he wear those tassel country vests and, like, drive an eighteen-wheeler for fun? Nobody. You play for the Jazz, things happen, man."

"Things happen everwhere," Pharaoh rasped. "Even Cleveland."

"Never picked up a gun till Utah," Belmont said sadly. "Now they want three games' pay."

The Pharaoh was staring into the fire. "I'm just sayin', we shouldn't shut ourselves out. This America. We want to try that country shit, we ought to."

Framed jerseys hung on the walls, where the moose and elk might have been, and I took the cognac Ras had given me and went into the shadows. Over the set of bronze fire tools was a

George Gervin, behind the humidor a Len Bias, and opposite the small library a Bulls-era Dennis Rodman. The shelves held at least two copies of *The Autobiography of Malcolm X*, and I wondered how Malcolm and the Worm would get on.

Ras came over, with the house's lone female servant trailing behind. He took on the air of a host in the evenings, as though it were his house to run so long as the Pharaoh was laying his purity aside. He was the cognac steward and dispenser of cigars, responsible for our pleasures, and, it would be seen, their consequences.

"You like de cognac?"

"It does taste like money," I said, holding it up with what felt like appropriate veneration.

He frowned. "It supposed to taste like gold."

I took another sip and my reply rang up in my ears with an unfortunate James Bondian quality. It was getting to be a strain to calibrate to Ras. His attitude toward me was one of paternal fraternity, which I was surprised to find I didn't resent—because he took me into his confidence, and he really did have all those polishes I hadn't even heard about. But sometimes I felt the awkwardness of trying to wear one mask over the other. I didn't know whether to reveal that I knew how the real masters did it, or the real servants. Any entry-level connoisseur knows your basic Hennessy is a sickly drink, but how could I get this across when what I was supposed to feel was the servant's gratefulness for being given anything at all?

"Was it Napoleon who liked Hennessy?" the woman asked.

"Courvoisier, Shida," Ras said in a flat, learned voice, like a historian of the haute, moving away as Pharaoh signaled him.

"I thought that was Busta," she chuckled, remaining.

"I thought you didn't talk," I said, looking curiously into her warm, dark eyes. Beyond Ras there were three other servants, all black. Maxim was a sort of butler and the daytime staff leader, and Wedge did all the outdoor work and made the espresso and was as tall as Pharaoh himself. Then there was this woman, Shida, who could make up my room expertly in about forty-five seconds, whose cooking was badly hit-and-miss, and whom I had never before heard utter a word.

"I talk," she said shortly. "I talk to people harmless like you."

"Busta's a Courvoisier guy, too," I said, like I'd made a chart of this all sometime back. "I'm not harmless, I'm just biding my time. Who's Hennessy got?"

"Hennessy got Kim Jong-il! Who else they need?"

"Okay okay," I said. "I'm writing this all down. Rémy got anybody?"

"Dre!"

"Rémy and soda pop."

"You judgin'?" she asked suspiciously. But still her eyes were laughing and dark.

"It's easy to disagree with Napoleon," I said. "I mean, if I don't want to eat a leg of lamb every day, that's fine too, right? But Dre . . ." In my mind I saw the rapper turning to me from the grainy videos I'd puzzled over the lyrics to in middle school, compelling belief, and then the squat, florid conqueror at his oaken table, mutton juice on his sleeves, looking like anything but a reliable judge of taste.

"Always easier to cross your own," she said, and I felt a strange rush at being instinctively understood.

The double doors swung open, and Goat and Odette came in. Her hair was damp and she was wearing a thick green robe. She seemed to exist in a constant state of going to or coming from the shower, and it was maybe this as much as anything that lent her the air of accidental provocation. She would put on a dress for every dinner, for an hour or two, and then it would be off again, on some pretext. Goat had changed into a black silk shirt, buttoned to the neck, and to talk to her he had to bend down cripplingly.

"And then as a sophomore I broke my foot," he was saying. "I broke my collarbone at Red Rocks. And of course I've sprained my ankles five or six times each, that happens to everyone. But that was all kid stuff next to the ACL."

She nodded up at him, then lifted her hand. "Look at my bruise," she implored. They went past.

"Have they been here before?" I asked.

"He hasn't. She comes and goes."

"Are she and Mr. Ramses . . . ?"

Shida scoffed and looked at me sideways.

"It's not like that," I said, not sure what I was denying.

She nodded wryly and the short, banded knots of her hair bobbed. "We don't ask. While he's here, Mr. Ramses prefers to live chastely. What happens in the city isn't our business."

"Nor what happens here," I reminded her, very noble, with what I thought was a flash of *Upstairs, Downstairs* inspiration.

She looked at me and made a little choking sound in her throat.

In the center of the room, Odette sat with Calyph on a tan leather couch. It had a faded, Western-looking throw over the back, and as I watched she lifted a corner and sniffed discreetly, as though it were full of the pungent musk of woodsmoke and men.

Odette still changed every room she graced, but after a day and a half the other guests were starting to get acclimated. Belmont still tried to ignore her, becoming involved in some game or conversation whenever she came near. The first night he'd roped Calyph into a game of dominoes on sight of her. Calyph soon got tired of it, leaving an opening, and to Belmont's obvious distress Odette had asked to be taught to play.

"I got to go to bed," he said, racing the dominoes back into the box, and then of course staying four more hours. Maybe Belmont was shrewd, and knew that by denying her so completely he was piquing interest. More likely he had a new wife.

By the first night she'd already broken Goat. He was docile, and held in her sway. Now he stood a little off, glancing at her with uncomfortable frequency. Pharaoh sat in his own chair, his back to the fire, eyes drooping but never closed. The skin on his forehead stood out in furrows too deep for a man who was all of about twenty-six. He was dark as French roast, and it looked like it withered him to be so tall and thin and black all at once.

Calyph had most nearly adapted to Odette. He acted amused all the time, and held his own. Whenever her flirting and uncertain relation to the Pharaoh caused a contagion of embarrassment, he looked not away but at her, and talked to her normally.

"You thought any more about your job?" he asked her now.

"Why would I?" she cried.

"I asked her today what she want to do with herself," he said, leaning over to Belmont. "She said she wanna be an art star."

"Huh!" Belmont said, making a big, square sound of it.

"I don't propose to discuss it with you."

"Art star," Belmont repeated. This phrase again stirred the sensation that I'd seen Odette somewhere before, but I still couldn't match her to a memory.

"And what would *you* be?" she pressed him. "If you didn't play?"

Calyph looked at her flatly, pretending to chew on something. "Rapper," he said, out of the side of his mouth.

"Come on!"

"Entrepreneur. Record producer."

"Don't mock me," she said, and for an instant her voice came out clear and strong. "What I want isn't anything like that."

He put up his hands for peace, and his pale fingers and palms had a sensitive look—they seemed to calm her. Still the Pharaoh looked on impassively.

"What does your wife do?" she asked him shrewdly, after a few moments had passed.

"Who?"

"Your wife. You have a ring," she said, pointing.

His hands flashed out, almost violently. The ring he still wore caught the light. "What?" he asked, louder.

She was flustered; she must have seen she was paining him. But her curiosity was implacable. "If you're not married, take off your ring," she told him.

He looked down and I saw him start to shake his head, but then he stilled himself, and only looked at the ground, bright-eyed, saying nothing.

Odette patted him on the shoulder gently with her wounded hand, on which the smallest two fingers were splinted together.

I hadn't heard anyone say Antonia's name in his presence for a month. He'd trained us; I hadn't heard him say it for two. When he learned of her other house, I got a voice mail from his mother out of nowhere, telling me to take a long weekend off. The weekend stretched for ten days, and I walked down through Jamison Square and past the early happy-hour crowds every night, like taking a walk was the new going out, and came home to watch the beginnings of the Brewers' wild-card run on the bachelor's tiny television. When I was finally called back to Dunthorpe, half the garage was filled with cat toys and old boxes meant to hold high-end cookware, and which now contained among them a few hundred cubic feet of Antonia's life.

The door in from the garage was ajar, and when I knocked the small sound flew through the empty space, as though her absence had opened the house up to new, desolate echoes. I couldn't find Calyph until I stepped out into the yard and heard him call down to me from the balcony in a flat, exhausted voice. All I could see were his hands, the nails bright where he gripped the rail. "Got some bags by the stairs," he said. "You gonna need a week's change. We goin' on vacation."

What followed were three grim days in Vegas, where Calyph met up with his best friend in the league, Tony Allen, to seek consolation in brotherhood and surface beauty and gambling and loss. It was clear from the first he was not going to find it. The nearest he seemed to get to solace was sitting at a poker table all night with his hood up and his leg splayed out on its own chair, ceaselessly shuffling his chip stacks and trying to ignore the continuous passive motion machine encasing his knee that he had to wear eight hours a day to help with his rehab. I wasn't much help with any of this, and he decided to send me home early.

On the last night before I flew back, after two days of sobriety, he and Allen split a fifth of scotch and some room-service sushi, and I pretended reluctance while they dragged me along for a limo ride down the Strip. Abruptly Calyph was happy, dangerously happy, lit up with the flashing, restless, ever-dissolving energy that is that city's promise to everyone. It came from everywhere but within him, and he must have felt almost obligated to go after his forty minutes of cathartic joy, juiced as it was with the premonition of its own passing and a return to his rightful state of sorrow with nothing but a new and more tangible pain in his head to console him. "I'm free," he said softly, addressing himself to the open window and the passing twilit city. "I'm free."

"You free," Allen said. "You'll get her back if you want her back."

"Who back?" Calyph asked.

"Don't say her name."

They'd brought along another fifth, and I had enough of it that whenever I breathed out my nose I felt like I'd inhaled a little of the North Sea. I felt full of solemn excitement and decided this was true of everyone. We drove through the city with no music in the car, going station to station with fleeting bits of other people's gaiety, and I decided all three of us were contemplating our futures. I wanted America's conception of how long youth could last to continue to recede conveniently beyond my aging, and yet also to stop so I could settle down swiftly and fulfill my promise. Calyph must have known his dreams of an All-Star Game were probably dead, but he knew that he could still aspire to a ring, and to matter in the getting of one. Maybe Allen was already thinking of where he would go after Boston. We all nodded slow at one another, as though to affirm my speculations, and my vague future seemed no less firmly possible than their specific ones.

We knew, I decided, that the fact that we were on the Strip in a big tasteless car without destination said nothing good about us, that this was, for the aging non-baller crowd, pretty much a painfully spring-break play, and for them surely something better savored when one was sixteen and in town for an AAU tournament, the cup of glitz still new on their lips. But we knew, too, that it was within us to justify this extravagance, to carry it right, with the weight of our accumulated actual lives and our allowance that, yes, we were poised delicately between the present eagerness to lose ourselves and the indisputable future likelihood of gradually becoming the wrong people, of failing at everything worthwhile, and absolutely knew it. In front of the Venetian, Allen threw up violently out his door. He swore it all still tasted good.

At the Pharaoh's, the night passed. Belmont and Goat played spades with a couple of the entourage, Goat laughing noisily at Odette's lisping jokes. Around midnight the host roused himself and called Calyph over to a sideboard, where Ras pulled out a plain decanter of dull metal. When he laid three stemless glasses on the polished wood, they rolled their way to rest like spinning tops. Ras poured and I watched Calyph take the liquor and swirl it around under his nose awkwardly, like a parody of a tony gent. I was relieved to see there was a culture to which he, too, aspired but didn't know the gestures for.

I saw Ras signal for me. I crossed the room and they put a glass in my hand.

"Let's take a walk," the Pharaoh said.

I didn't know whether to be honored or afraid, but I drank, and my willingness was sealed. The cognac was finer than what I'd drunk before, less sweet. I was given the metal bottle to carry—I knew its shape inside the black velvet bag, and I knew that what they'd given me, however fine, had come from somewhere else. Shida handed Calyph his crutches, and then the three of us were moving out of the room, and I felt buoyed by the curiosity of everyone left behind.

When we came out onto the terrace, the path through the darkness lit up in stages with blue running lights.

"Didn't press nothin'," Pharaoh said slyly. "It just know."

I walked behind them along the narrow stone path, and watched the rubber ends of Calyph's crutches plant on the flat centers of the wider stones. We moved out beyond the tent until the vast dark roar of the Pacific opened in front of us. The wind blew stiff down the north coast, and the moon lit up the whites of the waves, and, on the beach beneath, great strewn timbers and bits of scudding spume.

"Look at this shit," Pharaoh said softly. "It always doin' this."

"There it is," Calyph said. "There it go."

The sound of the sea rolled up and over us, timeless and elemental, the somehow reassuring noise of a crushing immensity patiently crashing against the human shore.

"Seem like every time I open up the house this gotta happen," Pharaoh said obliquely. "Somebody come and wanna drink liquor at five. Somebody show up with no girl and don't know which here is free and which not. Boys see a little structure to a thing and can't help theyselves but break it."

"It's his first taste in awhile," Calyph said. "He think he in a mansion video. Got that wild look in his eye like he about to turn the corner on that pool where the girls just stand around and jiggle, day after day. He forgot the rapper ain't own that mansion."

"Let 'em try to own one! Debauch the body all year and not put no rules to the thing. Sit by the pool and feel sick."

They were both quiet a minute, and I guessed each was ruminating on his first flush year, the brevity and disillusion of the supposed endless summer.

"I always invite too many people," Pharaoh croaked finally. "That's all it is. So what you think of my staff?"

"All good people," Calyph said carefully.

"Take what you want," Pharaoh said, and brought his glass to his lips.

Calyph was facing away, and I could only wonder how he took this blunt invitation. Once more they let the ocean swallow up their silence, and I turned the bag around in my hands. Its velvet and soft string made it feel like some particularly important object—a sack of gold or a prisoner's hood.

"We oughta be gods," Calyph said quietly, looking out at the sea.

"Ought?"

Calyph didn't reply. He looked out, and I could see maybe half his face, and somehow he had just the right balance there, in the cast of his eye and the set of his mouth. He looked noble, and it pained me. His face was equal to the vista and the question, and I wanted to mimic it, or else scrub it all out. It's the black Lewis and Clark, I wanted to shout.

"No ought to," Pharaoh said. "I made this. Somewhere there some boy in North Lawndale, restin' he head on bricks, on the side of a stoop, he can make this. We got to heaven, Yoshi. It's here. God's just some man who knows how to make laws for hisself. So he can stay in the place he made, and know it's good."

Calyph nodded, remotely.

"So listen here," Pharaoh said, louder, turning halfway away from the sea. I saw his eyes flash to mine. "You havin' a nice time here, I hope."

"Sure," I said. My voice felt rusted from disuse.

"Good. How you feel about looking after Mr. Montaigne a little bit? He don't have nobody, see. Yoshi and I been talkin', and he say he don't need you too much here. Shouldn't take much time. Whatchu say?"

"Okay," I said.

"See, Goat, he lost," the Pharaoh said sadly. His voice took on a new sensitivity, and I mistrusted it. "Might benefit him to have another boy to talk to. Tell him how we do here. Like we been sayin' just now—rules of staying in heaven and whatnot. What to talk on and whatnot. Who to dote on and who not. You having similar backgrounds and whatall, I thought you might could do it."

I wanted to tell him I'd not gone to Boise State, but to the Harvard of the Midwest, but of course I only nodded, as if this were all easy business.

"He know the code, right, Leef?" Pharaoh asked.

Still Calyph looked remotely out at the waves. "Far as I know," he said.

Pharaoh nodded, like this was good enough and we'd struck some definite deal. Raising his glass, he sent me back to the house, and I felt the swagger come up in my legs a little, for being confirmed a man of code. In the dark of the path I felt the fine strings of the bag loosen between my fingers, and lifted their bottle to drink.

I was taking my contacts out for the night when Calyph came crashing into the bathroom. I'd read for an hour or so, and then, disdaining the narrow utilitarian bath near my own room, gone upstairs to use the one on the main floor with the bronze fixtures and the raised copper sink.

"Hup to," he said, stumbling past me toward the toilet.

I had one eye out already. "Do you mind?"

"This the colored bathroom. Hup to," he said again, giving me a little push toward the door.

I wasn't about to stand there and watch him rain down, so I put my eye back in and went. Five minutes later all was silence.

I knocked softly. "You all right in there?"

Eventually I heard him clear his throat and come back to life. "Get in here," he said.

He was slouched on the closed toilet with his hands on his knees, wearing the blank, patient expression of a man waiting for something beyond his control.

"Drink some cognac?" I asked.

"Snuck up on me."

"Can you stand up?"

He thought on this. "Don't seem advisable."

"Let me help you," I said. "I used to work for a night doctor."

"A who?"

In retrospect I probably could have traded on my personal experience being too drunk to stand up, rather than inventing a more formal expertise. Still, I imagined a man with a private practice, catering to wealthy debauchees. He would make his rounds between midnight and dawn, carrying with him a black valise, coming to their bedsides after they'd incapacitated themselves and ministering to their indulgences with pills and IVs so that they could wake fresh and rested without fear of liver damage and resume their public lives with unnatural ease. He wore, I decided, a short Vandyke beard and pince-nez, and I had been his assistant.

"Let's get you to your room," I said. "You need to throw up first?"

He shook his head so hard it was like he was asserting a moral stance.

"Don't be proud. It helps."

"I'm straight," he said, so I went and stood by him. When he put his arm around me it seemed to weigh thirty pounds itself, and I felt a quiet triumph that I didn't crumple as he lifted himself to stand. Feeling hammered to the ground with every step, I helped him out the door to his nearby room, thankful that only Pharaoh and Odette slept on the highest floor.

I was surprised to see his room was hardly larger than my own. We came on the bed in the dark and I was expecting at least a perfunctory spaciousness near the door, but the mattress about took me out at the knees.

"Water," he muttered, shuffling away in the dim.

In the dark kitchen I could hear laughter through the walls, and I scrounged silently by the refrigerator bulb. I didn't want to be discovered and have to share the burden of him. I got some electrolyte water and fixed a plate of beans and cornbread, then went back to the bathroom for a single tablet of the right kind of painkiller. I added a few random vitamins, to show I had the professional touch.

When I got back he was sprawled out on the bed, epic in scale, pathetic in detail. His clothes were wrinkled and I could see the nubs on the backs of his socks. I knew that to nurse him as I would was yet another way of getting closer—I knew then it would be closer and closer always, after more and more control, and never enough. But it wasn't for the sake of that alone. I knew what I'd done to him. Every time his godhood slipped, every time he winced in a human way, I saw again the falling ice and the invisible wrenching of his ligaments; every time his face hurried to empty itself at the most oblique reference to Antonia, I felt my own casual hand driving them apart. I couldn't have known he'd take a little house so seriously. It seemed only right to help him put his life back together again. I might really mean something to him then, if I could do that. So when I woke him, and the cup touched his lips, I was in his service as purely as I knew to be. When the pills fell from his mouth, I was there to pluck them up again, and when he needed help with this clothes, I was there within his arms to lift them, serving and only serving.

6

The last night of our stay was the full moon after the equinox, the night of the hunter's moon. The night meant so many things in the Pharaoh's world, no one could keep count of them. For ease, the servants just regarded it as his own invented holiday, tied to nothing so much as his will to have it. The night almost marked the beginning of the regular season, and it almost marked Halloween. To a player on an active roster, the weeks of two-a-days and curfews and preseason games were over, and the future was writ large in games with stakes to them and post-victory nightlife and a holiday full of masked license, sexy versions of all the professions, and people who dressed up as everyone with a salable jersey, even you. That everyone kept confusing the day with the actual equinox seemed only to further our license to do anything.

Pharaoh did anything better than anyone. We woke on the day of the hunter's moon to find a champagne brunch. Goat appeared back in good standing, and the Pharaoh was telling him dirty jokes. All the rules we'd just had time enough to learn were broken. Odette had a dress on before noon and off by two, so all the really late risers mistook her evening pajamas for morning ones.

I drank a little bubbly with my coffee and eggs, and when I was called to help strike the video-game tent all my movements felt drifty. We packed the gear into carts, and Wedge directed a temp crew in raising a larger tent for the evening's festivities. It was striped red and black and green and had a hole in the middle to allow a fire. It was a perfect fall day, and when the pavilion was ready we couldn't sweep it clean for the yellow leaves that blew through, hushing over the shadowy stone and clinging in the fire pit, waiting for evening and the match that would turn them into light.

Goat hadn't required much attending. The afternoon after he was put in my care, I found him sprawled emotionally in the empty living room and asked if he'd like anything done to his car. He told me he'd been quoted several thousand for the dent on his fender, and asked if I could hammer it out. I could see he was lacking in what the Pharaoh would consider a firm code. That day he'd started in on the champagne hard, and I figured I only had eight or ten hours to head him off with a value system before it was too late.

The guests began to arrive around sundown. One by one, Maxim ushered them into the dining room, all the outlaw names of a gone era of Portland ball. There was Damon Stoudamire, who'd been caught with foil balls of marijuana in every major airport in the West, and Qyntel the dog-fighter, and Nick Van Exel, who had shoved a ref over the scorer's table in his younger days. Even Bonzi Wells came—Bonzi, who was thought to be the worst of them, though no one could ever remember anything really infamous he'd done. If Rasheed himself had walked through the door, shouting militant slogans, I couldn't have been any more excited. These were the Jail Blazers, assembled at the end of the nineties in a flurry of trades without regard for money or image or chemistry, only the fact that these men could jump a little higher, run a little faster, and make everybody who thought of a textbook layup as a timeless and important virtue cover their eyes with new and greater despair. At their peak they were the most talented team in the league, and but for a fourth-quarter meltdown in Game Seven of the 2000 Western Finals, they would have likely brought Portland their first championship since Bill Walton rode his bicycle to games and made all those things the bachelor believed about flowers and koans seem manly and tenable. But the collapse proved to a city that wanted to believe it that no amount of black talent could win a championship without heeding white virtues like disciplined back-cuts and modesty, virtues the city then demanded from the team and did not receive. The race war ran cold and unadmitted. For years, thousands paid the gate with bitter faces to come and boo their twelve former heroes and hope to get the finger from courtside so they could feel their animus justified. At last Wallace was traded—no one seemed to care for whom—and canned bells of jubilation rang out all night from the city's sports radio stations. Soon Portland had a team they could love again: awful, but beautifully docile.

One by one the Pharaoh embraced his old teammates, and pointed them to the buffet table where plateaued pyramids of gleaming rice flanked golden bowls of black beans and platters of jerk chicken and pork. I watched them go by me and felt a strange letdown at their failure to not give a fuck. I'd understood that it was important that they did not, that none be given, not to anyone who didn't stand up to their inscrutable scrutiny and pass the judgment of their obscure codes, formed in early years on back lots off streets so hard people like me could never hope to hear of them. For simplicity's sake, I'll say I assumed a fuck would certainly not be given to any white people. But now here these men were, a regular outlaw convention, and they just looked like some guys who dressed well and were excited to eat some dinner, and I was let down. I got in line behind them, and when Qyntel clattered a serving spoon back into the dish just outside my reach, he apologized in a soft voice.

In the pavilion the fire burned so high I thought the tent would catch. Already strange women were dancing in the firelight. Two had flat faces, and as I got near I saw they were wearing cardboard Bill Clinton masks. There was a cascade of masks lying on a green-clothed table next to the night's first flight of champagne, probably two dozen Bills and Hillarys, a Chelsea, and some Socks.

The dancing held a similar mix of the ritualistic and the improvised. Fits of unity saw the women join hands and clomp their feet together, but there weren't yet enough of them to circle the fire, and as I watched they seemed to decide they'd put on a respectable display of sisterhood and the circle dissolved into knots of ordinary clubbing. Joseph Jones didn't look impressed. He had a dapper tan suit and a dour, businesslike face, and I kept seeing him standing joyless at the edge of the light as the evening rushed on and wondering what had brought him there.

I heard a whistle, and saw Goat's bony arm rise in the flamy light. Next to him, Belmont lifted a champagne bottle and swung it like a sad pendulum.

"Bottle service," Belmont cried, and I brought them a new one. I tore the foil and loosed the wire cap, then held out the corked bottle.

"You do it," Goat said. "We'll put your eye out."

Grasping the neck, I gave the cork a sharp turn. The bones in my wrist cracked with alacrity and the bottle-smoke rose up.

"Gotta let it pop," Goat chided, pointing at the cork in my hand. "Let the ladies know we're here!"

"They know we're here, handsome," Belmont said.

"I can open another," I said.

They turned to one another. I'd meant this as a rebuke but they just looked inspired.

"That'd be wasteful," Belmont pointed out wistfully.

"'S'all right," Goat assured him. "We'll recycle 'em. Bring over another and get y'self a glass," he directed.

I got the bottle and watched Goat struggle with the foil. They'd begun at brunch and gone right through. I guess they'd been training for the rigors of this one way or another, as they were still semicoherent. The primary change in Goat was that his brooding sensitivity seemed to have been replaced by an aggressive forwardness that carried with it an indefinite change in dialect.

"Bel and I were just talkin'," Goat confided. "They treat you folks real nice here."

I nodded out our cumulative gratitude.

"Ram treat his people right," Belmont said.

Goat threw the balled foil off into the trees. "You better watch it, though," he said, pointing a wavering finger at me. "They're coming for that cush job of yours."

"How's that?"

"Pharaoh already tried to hit me up once to get one of those Jones boys to do some work for me. One of them refugees. Why do you think we're here? It's like when they give you a free vacation in Hawaii but then they're all over you to buy a yacht or something."

We both looked over to Belmont for confirmation, but he just laughed.

"Imagine you with a servant, living outta yo trunk! I mean, I seen Joe here tonight, but nobody hit me up for shit yet."

"Maybe Calyph will stay loyal," Goat said. He turned back to me abruptly. "If not, though, better grab a piece tonight on your way out. Bet you could."

"How's that?" I asked again, just to be companionable, and reached to take a drop from the bottle.

"Odette's going off tonight," he said. "Just be in the vicinity!"

His eyes were wide and a little uncertain, like he was striving to convince himself his excitement had a basis.

Belmont hissed through his teeth and looked around doubtfully.

"It's true, Bel. I know her type."

"She don't got a type. I best stay clear of all that."

Goat worked the wire loose at last. "That serving girl looks nice, too. What's her name?"

Belmont rubbed his hand over his small, close-shaven head. "Unless Pharaoh, like, offers you somethin', Luke, I'd keep off that, too. You don't know how he feels about them doing what with who."

"That's true," I said, seeing an opening for my wisdom at last. They both looked over at me strangely, as if this were the opinion of a new, fourth party.

Goat spat through his teeth in defiance. "I think it'd be all right. We're his guests here. Besides, you ever see how he, like, points 'em at us, almost?"

Belmont scoffed. "Be honest? All I see is your gapin' face."

"Is that what you see?" Goat put one of his knobby hands in front of his mouth, pressing his knuckles against his teeth. His eyes seemed to screw up and grow smaller. "Bel, I know what I am. I'm that man who got cast outta the palace. Now I just wander around the land in my beat-up car, trying to get my broke body right, trying to find a way back in. Into that sweet life I knew. But Pharaoh, he took me in here, and I'm grateful. I don't want nothin' that's his. Just, a girl's what tells you you had a sweet time. A girl's what tells you what you should remember." His singsong lapsed, but his face was still alive with the bright determination to show us he knew something hard-won and inarticulable.

Silently we drank from our golden cups, until he recovered himself.

"Maybe that Shida's all right," Belmont said. "All I'm sayin' is, if he pointin' Odette around, I'm a damn Latter Day."

I gave an extra-strong nod to this. Goat frowned at me like he was yielding the point but wanted us to know that all this prudence oppressed him. He sighed. "See," he said, shaking the unopened champagne lightly. "You gotta foam the bottle. When you open it, everybody looks, they wanna see some foam come out. Makes 'em feel like they won somethin'."

He stood and popped the cork off into the night, and a spurt of foam fell dripping onto the stone.

"Champions of the world," Belmont said softly.

I went away and stood at the edge of the light and watched the dancing. Ras had joined the floor, the first man, doing a spry, unassuming shuffle near the two Clintons. Nearby, Shida too had begun to dance. She moved like a dervish, scything the air. She was hypnotic to watch because nothing she did showed she wanted to be seen. The grace seemed to be happening for its own sake, for her own joy, rather than to call attention. There was even something of her usual reserve that clung to her, in spite of her exact, dynamic steps. She danced so sure, but toward the edge of the light, as if practicing, brushing the dust off stores of moves. She might have been alone.

I felt a strange attraction to her, unpossessive and detached. I couldn't find anything to compare it to. With no intention of dancing, I went and stood by her. As soon as she saw me she stopped cold.

"What's up, harmless?" she asked.

"Nothing," I said.

"Okay." She dipped her shoulder and turned smoothly back into her solitary, scything dance.

After a few steps she turned back, with as much abrupt grace as before, and stopped again, dead.

"You still here," she laughed.

"Yeah."

She turned up her hands helplessly. "Let's sit down, I guess."

We took seats on the Pharaoh's chaise, which had been pushed into an empty corner of the pavilion and strung with two balloons that nudged together, looking like failed fun. The glare from the bonfire tapered into dim and we could see out at everyone moving through the smoke.

"Funny old night," she said. "VIP Halloween."

"Dead players rise. Servants become masters."

"How you figure?"

"It's a masked dance, right? That means we lose our identities for the night."

She laughed. "Even with a Bubba on, you still the only short white guy for miles."

I straightened enough to look down at her and she rolled her eyes. We gazed out at the backlit whirl of lanky figures, the towering men and thin, careful women. I thought I saw some of the old players join the dance at the far edge of the light, their figures wavering in the heat.

"Seriously, though," she pressed. "We still the help. Stay harmless. Don't go misbehaving with anybody important."

I looked curiously at the flashing whites of her eyes. The air was full of warnings, and then I wondered if this was an invitation to misbehave with the unimportant. "This your first one of these?"

"I've only been here nine months."

"What did you do before?"

"If I told you I used to be on the dance team, would you laugh in my face?"

I laughed silently in her face, until my own froze with realization.

"You and Pharaoh?"

She looked at me fiercely. "You think pretty high of dancers!"

"So you didn't?" I figured there must have been some court-ship, but her face broke out into further indignation.

"When I met him, mufucker was drivin' a car with Ben Frank-lin painted on the hood—Ben smokin' a spliff rolled up with a hundred. I turned him down till he thought his number was no. You think I'd still be here, with Odette here, if I said yes? Shit . . ."

"Well, you probably made it with some of the other guys," I said soothingly.

"Don't think I won't slap you now," she said, half raising her hand in the dark.

"I've never been slapped."

I caught the hint of a new smell and then the side of my face broke out tingling. The heel of her hand caught me on the jaw and I felt an ache shiver down my neck and one of my vertebrae crack. I wanted to shake loose the clouded, jarred feeling, but I held my face still, so she'd have to wait for my response.

I stared and she stared back, eyes alight with furious amuse-ment.

" 'Woman! You crazy?!' " she mocked in a hard whisper.

I was looking at the balloons over her shoulder, feeling the pleasure of the slap, and the delight that would come from beating her with them in revenge, harmlessly, when I heard a dry *hunh* of a chuckle and sensed figures looming. I was put in shadow; the fire was blotted out.

"Hit him some mo'," somebody said.

She flinched and drew herself away.

"White boy, every time I see you, you gettin' hurt," said the nearest loomer. I looked up at the thickset blotch of him and tried to remember who this was, who even in commiseration seemed angry.

"You know this chalk?" the first voice asked.

"I seen this chalk shot with a flare," the near man said. "I seen this chalk get just about melted, man."

It was the man from the crap game. Ordinarily I might've been pleased to be remembered by someone so antithetical to myself, even if it was just for being shot. But they'd come up and broken into a privacy I wanted to prolong.

"Is this guy bothering you?" Goat said idiotically, meaning me.

"He okay," Shida said. "I was just showing him how to do that."

"You wan show me, too?" said the first man, who had called me a chalk, a thin anonymous figure with an entitled drawl. In the dim he looked like the universal ballplayer, so without memorable characteristics he'd need to wear a special headband or elbow sleeve to distinguish himself.

They all went quiet, waiting for her answer. I watched her, feeling shouldered aside, wanting her to say she only slapped me, but she seemed to find the situation familiar, and I watched a look of resignation flit across her face.

"Okay," she said, and suddenly stood, and I watched in disbelief as her arm bent back and her open hand flew out.

The thin man caught her by the wrist and held her, watching her carefully. He laughed his dry *hunh* of a laugh, once. Then he just took her away. I couldn't believe she would really go. Her arm remained fully extended, like a proud prisoner, but she walked along behind him. The rest of the group turned and trailed after the couple, Goat striding excitedly to keep up.

"I can't slap all you," I heard her say.

Somebody told her she could try.

As they moved away, I saw Belmont was with them, and he turned to me a moment with what must have been sympathy.

"But I was talking to her," I said.

"You could come, too. But it's best you don't." And then he melted away and was gone.

I stood and looked around at the laughing, cordial faces of the drinkers who had stepped aside for this rough procession. I felt my face screw up in judgment and in condemnation of them, of their automatic politeness that did not know what it was condoning, yet I felt paralyzed but to condone it myself, by my own uncertainty about what would happen to her, and her resignation to it. The fire stung my face, the roaring pyre turning before my eyes from a festive backdrop into the killing, consuming element it had always been.

I needed to see Calyph. In his absence he seemed a slumming angel who would know this moral terrain surely and instantly, and I wandered the estate after any sign of him with a glass in my hand, and then another, feeling only sicker and more sober with each drink. I went out to the cliff and found no one and looked down at the obliterating waves. Coming back again, I ended up by the fire at the table with the masks. Feeling by that point that my knowledge of the secret going on up in the house, in some bed in some little room, had disconnected and banished me from the society of the party, I put on the mask of the Clinton family cat, hoping to be comforted.

The two women came past with their own masks pulled up flat on top of their heads.

"Socks!" they said.

"Yeah, yeah," I said. "Have you seen Calyph?"

"Who?"

"The basketball player."

"Ha-ha," one said.

"Be more specific, cat."

I opened my mouth against the flat of the mask with further

impatience but felt a strange blankness in my mind. I could not describe him.

"He needs a haircut," I said finally. "He's proud. When he laughs he looks crazy."

They looked back at me blankly.

"The injured one," I said.

"Oh," they both said swiftly. But they shook their heads.

"Come back, Socks," they called after me. Stumbling beyond the edge of the light, I almost bumped into Joseph Jones, who sat primly at a wrought-iron table in the gloom, a thick binder open in front of him as if he were auditing the party. He frowned at me, and as soon as I was by him I peeled off my mask and tossed it away.

When I could wander no longer, when there was nowhere left to go but after her, I squared myself and went slowly back toward the house. Lit from within with soft and ordinary light, it had a solid and almost monastic look after the pavilion. Walking toward it, I tried to instill in myself the hope that I was moving out of the backyard wilderness into a more ordered world.

The whole main floor was empty. In the dining room, the food lay covered in its dishes, present only in its smell. In the white living room, a pot of tea sat next to two clean glasses. I cupped the pot and it warmed my hand.

Then he came up the stairs, from where our rooms were, buttoning his cuffs, the universal player. I straightened and moved toward him, looking for signs, for scratches on his neck or who knew what, but he looked only bored and flawless and entirely composed.

"'Sup, chalk," he said, and nodded as he went past, moving without slowing, acknowledging and dismissing me in one gesture, out toward the wilderness.

And then I heard voices from below. Even as they broke out

in argument I was moving, and yet as soon as I saw Ras appear he was speeding toward me and past me already at an impossibly brisk walk.

"Do not come down heah," he said in a loud, fussy voice. "Do not come down."

Below in the low, narrow hall, Belmont leaned against the wall opposite a closed door, frowning. As I watched, Ras took him by the shoulder, then stood in front of the door, angrily composing himself. Inside it was quiet but for a heavy jerking sound, like a bed being moved by two people who disagreed about where to put it.

"We told him it won like that," Belmont said. "She okayed the first brother, you know? We told him you can't just go in. You gotta wait for her to say. But he didn't wanna hear it."

"Just go, please," Ras said. "Just please go back to de party and enjoy yourself."

He straggled away, troubled but reprieved, too willing, and I followed him out of the hall and then stopped around the corner.

I heard Ras take a last square breath, making himself ready, and then the knob of the door turned and I heard three voices rise up all at once, protesting one another, the men arguing indistinguishably beneath a woman's sudden, powerful, repetitive cry of no. It didn't go on long—what was there to argue, next to that cry—but the man inside the room demanded his say, and so a dispute sprang up, and continued even out into the hall, as Goat limped past me shirtless and smelling of fresh rubber, bleeding from the ear and pulling with all the dignity he could summon at his loose unbelted slacks. As Ras shoved him along, Goat was using, in the maintenance of his own defense, the same phrases he had so recently come to favor, between bottles of champagne, as organizing principles for his life as it culminated in parties, that this, just this, this was how you knew you had a sweet time, this was how you knew what to remember, and even after I lost sight of him, herded away in the passage toward the pool, he was still doggedly negotiating the prospect of being allowed to return.

I crept up to the dark, half-shut door, listening. I wanted to go in but the bitter smell in the air repelled me.

Inside, a lamp clicked on, and in the sudden light I pushed through. She was sitting in bed, clothed, opening a book. She looked at me firmly, as if willing me to accept the normalcy of this scene, and I could think of nothing to say or even to look back at her. I just stood. She wore a loose turtleneck sweater and an overlarge pair of square, plastic-framed glasses. There was only the bitter rubbery unmentionable smell of aftersex thickening the air.

"Fun's over," she said finally.

I went and sat at the end of the bed.

"You think you gonna hold my hand through this?" she asked. "We got people for that."

"Let me see that book," I demanded.

She handed it over with a scornful look, but readily. It seemed to relieve her a little not to be pitied, to fulfill a simple and immature demand. The novel was some historical Mormon thing about somebody's twenty-seventh wife or so, and I flipped dismissively through its pages. I read it for a few minutes, making a show of it. I was deeply pained by its every imagined transgression. She wanted to read her way back to normalcy and I hoped to do my part.

"I wish we could have kept talking before," I said.

"Yeah."

"I was going to whup you with those balloons."

"I'd have slapped you again."

"Do you want to?"

There didn't even seem to be time for her to parse the question before I felt her palm again and my face break out tingling. I looked up at her, amazed.

"I'm sorry," she said. "Was that like rhetorical?"

"No," I said, and she slapped me again on the other side.

"Okay," I said.

"Your glow's balanced now," she told me. "Don't that feel better?"

"Take it out on me," I said. "Whatever you got."

She looked at me flatly. I was not even in the same world as her trouble. "I took it out on him. I about ripped his nutsack open. He didn't even get it in, weak little crooked-dicked bitch. Now gimme my book."

I heaved it at her carelessly and it splashed against her knees. Again I saw her palm flash out, but this time I was just ready enough to deflect her enough to get hurt, and her nail raked the corner of my mouth. I felt my head jerk in surprise, and my hand shot up, all out of proportion, as though to ward off permanent disfigurement.

"Poor baby. Did I hurt you?"

I tongued the spot and tasted blood.

I felt her hand again on my face, tenderly now, brushing my lip. Her face was poised beyond the blockade of her wack glasses. I heard the air going in through my nose loudly.

"The white man's skin . . ." she began, like she was narrating a nature documentary. "Feel like a newspaper nobody wanna look at."

Her fingers traveled on, pressing lightly on my cheek. Her eyes were curious and unafraid, as though she were making a purely scientific inquiry. I felt myself holding my breath, in order to still myself, that I too might be controlled to this point of delicate sensitivity. I felt myself submitting to the scrutiny of her sad, almost pitying eyes and the touch of her impersonal fingers. I felt understood.

And then a strange, ripe smell caught in my nose. Her fingers brushed across the pores on my inner cheek, and I smelled faint spices from her cooking, but beneath, at the heart of the smell, there was something rank, something rotten or raw, as though the odor of bad meat had been pushed into the pores of her fingers, or that caught within her nails was some bit of pork fat. The bitter stink of aftersex from the first man again flooded my nose, smelling like rubber and the absence of love.

The smells seemed to join together in her then. They seemed to be coming from her very skin. I gave a hard involuntary cough. I'd never been that near to a black woman before—perhaps that was just how they smelled. I coughed again, and I saw her sadly curious eyes widen and then focus, and she leaned back swiftly, her face questioning and flattening already into defensive derision.

"Boy, you think this is that? After him?"

I sat there a moment, smelling her. I could feel it acrid in my nose. I exhaled, trying to suppress my revulsion, thinking of my own stink, of Calyph's sweat, of all the smells that had been pressed into her that night but her own. But I couldn't get any hold on myself. That's how they smell, some part of me whispered. I stood and turned away.

"I'll be right back," I said, but I just left her there.

I felt a desperate need to wash my face, but the bathroom on the servants' floor was occupied—as a detainment center, I guessed, for I could hear Ras's low voice from within. Dazed, I wandered on, toward the pool, picking up a towel from the stack with the vague notion that in submerging myself altogether I could become so cleansed as to have my instinctive responses altered, so I was no longer revolted by the very blackness in her that was what drew me to their men. It had always been there, I knew, that fear, that a black woman should want me, or even just let me close to her, unrealized only because of the utter whiteness of my world. I thought of Shida's nose and the texture of her hair, and how when she bent over I saw her as a fieldworker, and felt all the narrow, frowning men of my lineage, their faces behind my face, angry and impotent and wasted, men gone from the earth and the earth better for it, myself the last of this dying fallacy.

The poolroom was darker the higher you looked, the walls wavering in the upcast of its submerged lights. The rock wall where earlier in the week the Pharaoh had led an afternoon of cliff diving was pocked with black that glistened like volcanic glass, and beyond the pool a curtain of steam hung still above a raised stone tub. I was about to strip off my shirt when I heard a sneeze.

I edged forward until I could just see through the steam. Odette was sunk deeply in the tub, the ends of her loose hair floating around her, the water lapping at her throat.

"It's you," she said, the words echoing rounded and childish.

"Shouldn't you be at the party?"

"They don't need me tonight," she said, the lisp filtering coolly out of her voice. "I'm just for when there's nothing better."

I stood before her with the mist around me, wishing I was more compelling. I could almost feel her trying to summon some interest as she stared up at me.

"You're bleeding," she said suddenly. Her hand came out of the water and I could see the straps of a demure, black-and-white one-piece.

"I'm a man of violence," I told her.

"It's very soothing in here."

I kicked off my shoes just to see how we would feel about it, and then I went from there. I got down to my undershirt and trousers and decided it was far enough. The trousers had been torn a little that day I'd been flared and I was grateful to be seeing them to their ruin. Throwing the clothes to the ground, I felt a flash of disdain for myself, at my relief in settling back so immediately into unexamined lust for my own people.

I'd stepped up on the platform when I saw a second towel and a wallet laid out beyond her own discarded things.

"Who's that?" I asked, sliding into the water.

"Who?" she asked innocently.

My foot brushed hers a moment beneath the water and she kicked out at me playfully. "It's only me," she said.

Watching my shirt pull away from my skin and bubble with the surface, I leaned back and tried to look comfortable. As I stretched my legs out I could feel hers entwine with mine—it was like the sight of my blood had announced a new physical magnetism.

"Who hurt you?"

"Some lady," I said, knowing this was the right answer.

"There's just one drop, and it doesn't fall. It gets bigger but it just hangs." She reached out and touched my face. No one had ever liked to touch me and suddenly I was irresistible. She put her wet hand on my chin but avoided the wound, which she seemed to revere.

"Have you ever been married?" she asked suddenly.

"I haven't even been born yet," I told her.

"Really?" Her eyes lit in admiration. "I bet you're the oldest person here but me."

"You?"

"Look," she said. She lifted herself a little out of the water and ran her hand over her side where the suit curved away. As the skin pulled taut, two stretch marks purpled out.

She held the fabric back for me to touch the marked skin. I traced my finger across, but I couldn't feel anything.

"They're all children," she pronounced. "But they've already lived full lives, and we're gray and wrinkled and full of potential."

She smiled at me, wryly. When she spoke again her lisp had dried up entirely, and her voice was cool and exact. It was an affect, and it was shocking to hear this honed, grown woman's voice. She seemed almost a different person.

"We had a fight, Savier and I, about marriage. We talk about it all the time, but I know he won't. He says it's me; he says I always want other people. But I don't. If I was set up I could just let all that go by. What can I do but give myself to someone, before I get old? I know it won't work, it won't make me happy forever. I know we'll end up in hate. But I'll do it just the same."

Slowly she submerged herself. For a moment she peered up at me through the water's churn, and I knew I'd seen her before after all, on some pinup website. She was on a gray beach much like the one beyond the walls. There were about thirty pictures of her, in which she was captured walking down to a rocky shore in what looked to be an icy spring dawn, wearing a simple black dress. Her hair was much longer then, and black—it must have been her goth phase. What made the pictures most memorable drew the focus off her: the errand captured in the photoset was the "walking" of a puppy, made of bones. It looked like a done-up veterinary skeleton, leashed with a red ribbon and set off through the chill dew as though it were a necromancer's best friend, and she casually possessed of a few of the more fashionable black arts. Toward the sea they went, in somber procession, stopping here and there so she could scratch behind its vanished ears and carefully dry its feet. As the pictures progressed, the bone puppy led her to the beach and then down, stone by stone, to the edge of a tidepool. In the last photograph she stared up at the camera from beneath the water, clutching the puppy to her chest. By then the set had become a full nude.

She looked up at me then as she had looked at all of us, all the round world of men, through the tidepool. The world was full of naked people getting older. It was true, what she said: in the presence of men who'd been tracked in scouting magazines since the fifth grade, who'd been the new names shouted by overexcited color guys during thawing March days, when I was feeling really sort of a big deal now for having got a prime slot on college radio, one felt older, like talent already wasted. Our eyes were failing, our spines were curling in, soon we would be thirty, and thirty-five; we were graying in the womb of our undefined future excellence. To love sports, to love music, to love how young women in blinding bloom sat on old gray rocks and opened their arms, was to live in a world where it got late early. The sunken-eyed coach only now approaching mastery, the craggy composer of the sublime concerto, became irrelevant; how unhappy they looked, for all their wisdom, like they scratched their balls and got ashes on their fingers, on this elemental earth next to which even our ancience is fleeting. But, oh, old enlightenment, your business is nice, but while a man can yet jump so high his breath snuffs a candle on the back of the rim, while Odette unfolds her arms, then, old enlightenment, go somewhere and wait for us to need you, we will live forever as long as this lasts.

When Odette surfaced within my arms and kissed me for reasons too remote to protest, this vision had put me pretty well at my ease, and I had no trouble at all catching her by the shoulders and pushing her against the stone edge of the tub. She clasped my head wetly with both hands, to hold me still, and it was like a child's need for assertion, to set the rules of play, and so I pressed into her, and would not let her lead. We battled like that for a while, and then I took her wrist and dragged it pinned against the stone, just for fun. Looking up I saw it was the splinted hand.

"You're rougher than you look," she said huskily, turning her head aside. She put her hand over my face, and as her fingers spread I closed my eyes and she pressed lightly on my lids.

"You like it," I said automatically, because it had always been so.

"What if I don't?" she asked, making her voice small.

"Suck it up then, I guess." I pushed my face into her hand to see if she would hold me off. I felt her fingers drag luxuriantly away.

I went at her neck a bit, very chaste, careful to leave no mark, but with energy, leaving behind a faint streak of my own blood. She clutched me to her and began to speculate.

"You're one of those servants who thinks they're better than their masters," she said, chuckling lowly. "Usually you're very uptight."

"You smell like food," I told her, just to balance things. It wasn't true, but along the tub's edge I'd seen a plate of left-over beans and chicken bones. She stiffened a little, and then we heard the echo of steps.

For a long moment I thought it would be the Pharaoh, but his gait was wrong, misshapen—instead of casual steps we heard the squeaking, half-mechanical shuffle of the recently invalid. The hospital sounds of him seemed a judgment of their own, and as he came toward us through the mist Odette drew quietly away.

I didn't know how to face Calyph that way. It wasn't that I was ashamed, or had any feeling of having misbehaved. I was proud to be found out in her company, yet I felt outed some-how, uncomfortable at the revelation of my desires even where they were most universal. Again I lay back in the water, trying to be easy. I watched him loom up in the light and take us in. I remember hoping he'd see her as an unexpected wrinkle of me, a hidden prowess.

"You shouldn't be here, J," he said right off.

"Why?" I asked lazily, hearing my voice calibrate itself to some libertine cadence in the lone drawled word. I would've been glad to be treated almost any way, as a rival even, rather than to be given more stern warnings.

"You know," he said, and there was real heat in his voice. He didn't look at Odette, but still she shrank away, fading into the background as far as she was able. She'd lowered herself into the water so the purse of her lips lay along the waterline.

"Did I take your place?" I asked, hearing again the strange caress in my voice. "You forgot your wallet."

"I was here," he said, "before she was here. Then I got out. As you best."

Odette seemed to have sunk lower yet, intently watching us, her whole mouth submerged.

"It feels nice in here," I said. "Isn't it nice, Odette?"

"Yes," she lispered.

I felt all at once in total command of the situation and all parties in it. "You ought to join us," I said. "I'm sure Puma would like it."

She rose up in the water then, just slightly, so that her hair came dripping clear, watching him, waiting.

He hesitated a moment, and I could see he did desire her. I wondered if she'd told him about her fight with the Pharaoh. If he was true to his code it wouldn't have made any difference, but still he lingered, and did not look at her, and after all she was one to turn men's rules for themselves into just so much false dignity, so many resolutions left behind in a drawer somewhere at the moment of crisis, and I knew he knew it. Yet my own presence must have baffled and unnerved him—I was curious which force would be the stronger.

I imagined him stripping off his brace and lowering himself down, the water in the tub rising, bracing for our negotiation of one another as two bodies in the close space. How could we resist her, yet how could either of us touch her with the other there? How would she react to our mutual presence? I imagined she would be for it. All at once I imagined us both going for her, his hands and mine around her, feeding on her lips and limbs, our heads banging accidentally together. His scarred, shrunken leg would lie awkwardly against mine beneath the water; my blood off her would mark his face. I felt the sudden urge to clutch her, to hold her up to him. Full once more of the thrill of becoming unknown to myself, I grabbed her thigh to turn her toward him.

I watched him lower himself upon the crutches, and he leaned his face down to mine.

"You do what you want now, Jess," he said quietly. "This some sorry shit, though, you want to know the truth." Then he straightened and swung himself slowly away through the silent, dripping room.

As he receded I could feel her coming back to me. "It's all right," she tried to begin.

"Shut up," I said.

She sank herself into me a moment, obediently. Then she rose again and put her face in front of mine. "You're one of those white deviants," she pronounced, looking at me with mock-horror with a sort of approval breaking through it, as though she'd found in me something more interesting than expected.

I felt my lip curl at this. I thought tiredly that I'd better play along, just for an instant, that this deviance was something I ought to suggest an affinity for, so I could transcend it.

"Naw," I said. "Naw."

"No?"

"I got a little black in me," I told her.

She looked at me close; with soft fingers she examined my hair.

"You poor thing," she said.

I looked at her fiercely, willing her belief and, I was sure, its consequence, her envy.

"You poor, poor thing," she repeated.

I fondled her carelessly then—I turned her and once more pressed her against the stone of the pool. The fun seemed to have gone out of it a little, but I gripped her by the scruff of the neck and willed it back.

"Close your eyes," I said. "Turn your head."

She frowned but she did it.

"Keep them closed," I ordered. "Now open your mouth."

Her face was set in a thrill of dislike, but she'd decided this deviance I was supposed to have was attractive, a force to be obeyed. Her mouth opened slightly, warily, the corners of her lips peeling apart.

Rising up, I reached over to the edge of the tub and took the chicken in my hand. It was cool and greasy. I felt a shudder of disgust, but there seemed such a logic in what I was doing. It was like an inspiration of wrong. I put the fleshy end of the chicken bone to her lips.

After that I do not remember, only that we were on our feet in the spray and she was blazing at me, and I was trying to comfort her, to change her mind about me, absurdly to show her all the flair and daring of the act, how brave I was to carry through, knowing its repugnance.

"See," I kept saying. "No, look."

But she only blazed out. I don't remember if I was hit—the

marks would have been obliterated by the marks of what came after. I only remember pleading what a childlike, innocuous, not-worth-telling-anybody time we'd had, and then just trying to get out of there, to get her to let me go quietly, but then I heard more steps, and saw Joseph Jones through the mist, and Ras too, and Goat. It seemed they were trying to keep Goat from coming in, but when they saw me they put away their differences.

PART
THREE

7

On my twenty-eighth to last day, just as my bruises were at their most vivid, I drove out to Dunthorpe and Ras answered the door. There was a tin of polish in his hand, and he frowned a little when he saw me. He twisted the lid, ensuring its tightness, and I got the sense that with that gesture his trove of professional advice was closed to me forever. "From now on, de car stays heah."

"How do I get here?" I asked.

He pointed past me to an old Mazda parked at the edge of the driveway. The white crescent of nail at the tip of his finger looked cut to exactly one thirty-second of an inch all around. "For de rest of de month, dat is yours. Keep it clean or you will hear about it. Dent it and it comes out your wage."

From his pocket he produced a key on a long, yellow lanyard. The length of cord was a humiliation in itself, and I wondered if he would order it around my neck.

"What kind of driver don't have his own car!"

Getting into the thing, I slammed the seat back as far as it would go. The engine started with an ugly sound. I took it to the garage, and the car felt too light, too near the ground—it was as if I was piloting some child's kart. I took the spot farthest from the door, where Antonia used to park her scooter. Even the door handles felt flimsy.

Ras met me again at the door. "Now I'll show you your room," he said.

"My what?"

"I hope you brought a day's change."

"I don't understand," I said.

"Den you should just nod and smile," he said, leaning forward a little. "I cannot believe you do not know dese basic tings."

He walked past me to a door in the back wall I'd never seen open. The recycling carts that'd stood in front of it had been moved away, and I could see the faint lines of broom tines on the concrete. He opened the door and I saw a handrail slanting upward.

I looked at the ceiling. I couldn't understand there being anything above the garage. The roof slanted up on one side, but I thought that was just, you know, architecture. The garage ceiling was lined with planks, spaced inches apart, through which you could see the emptiness above, but atop my new car the space above the planks was covered over in particleboard. Ras had gone away up the stairs; his shoes sounded harshly on the cheap steps.

At the top of the stairs was a cramped room with a low, slanted ceiling. A single tiny window gave a grimy view of the Japanese garden. The room held a card table, folded up and leaning against the wall, a folding chair leaning in front of it, and, in the middle of the room, a rolling metal bed frame, also folded up, with a meager mattress sandwiched inside. There was a large pitcher in the corner. The pitcher wasn't folded up.

"It has de Internet," Ras announced in a jolly voice.

I felt the slant of the ceiling brush my hair. There was no hope of standing upright except against the far wall.

"You want to quit?" Ras asked. "Hmm? Dis is beneath you?"

"I want to serve out my time," I said.

"Good," he said, coming to the doorway and waiting for me to step aside. "Den make yourself at home, and wait."

I pulled out the chair and sat, dazed, feeling a voluntary hostage. I touched my yellow eye, and the spectacular mottle on my side where Savier had punched me above the kidney, disgustedly, exactly once. Ras and Joseph Jones had dragged me still wet from the tub down the same hall Ras had just pulled Goat along, and the Pharaoh was waiting in front of my little room.

Jones had given me the shot on the eye, for illustrative purposes or just for sport. "See?" he said. "You see what he is?"

The Pharaoh seemed impatient to get back to his party, and punched me hard without remark. They threw me in my room and I lay there until dawn, the chlorine itch spreading slowly across my body.

I picked up the pitcher and held it in my lap, putting my palms around its curve. The ceramic was warm, and it seemed the only friendly object in the room. Within my reach at the top of the stair was an intercom housed in the wood. The hole was bigger than the speaker, and I could see the stud behind and the wires going away down the wall. I wanted to press talk and see if I could get Calyph; I wanted to locate some reminder of my dignity. I turned up the volume, just to see if anything could be heard.

"What?" a distorted voice swiftly asked. It sounded like Wedge or Maxim. I turned the knob back, but in a moment the voice returned. "Don't come in the house," it said. "You ain't allowed in the house no more."

I rose and unbundled the bed and lay on it blankly. An indefinite time later I was woken from my daze by a shriek of feedback. "This shit on? Yo, Jess."

I stumbled over to the stair.

"How you like your room?" he asked. "We thought it'd be more convenient this way. They do it up right?" I couldn't tell if he was being flip or not, and looked at the plastic grille as though it might be of help.

"You got the wifi hooked up in there?" the speaker asked.

"Not yet," I said. I think I hoped he'd come up and check on the airwaves, and see my situation and be appalled.

"Ras put encryption on that mess, but we'll get you the code. Lotta changes around here I guess. Can you come down in about twenty?"

"I guess I can make that," I said.

After our last night at the Pharaoh's, we stopped at a seafood place on our way out of town. We got as far as the lobby, where a wooden sign hung with nets and rigging proclaimed famous clam chowder. Calyph's crutches stilled and he shook his head. He must have thought it too tacky a place to fire me in, and we turned around to find our fate on the public boardwalk. We ended up sitting on a sandy concrete slab by the sea, where I was given my thirty days' notice.

Thirty days! He had his moments of cruelty, his dictatorial sunglasses, and what his Hollinger profile called a mercurial persona, but Calyph was mostly too kind. Anyone with a less complicated relationship to his pride would've been able to fire me on the spot. He wasn't going to have to search very hard for a new driver—Joseph Jones had brought three newly trained servants with him to the Pharaoh's. I'll always be curious if he'd stowed them somewhere during the night, when I was stumbling around under the illusion that the world had suspended its moral judgment because the moon was full and somebody had brought a few masks, or if they had all filed in quietly at dawn, at the very moment the cognac glasses were taken away. So as not to breach taste, Jones treated them as his own attendants, but I knew that one of the dapper men avoiding my gaze as I took down Calyph's bags was my eventual replacement.

We sat on the slab and watched a bunch of children fly kites shaped like dragons and butterflies, until a kid wearing a hemp necklace came over and handed Calyph a marker and a soccer ball.

"I got Travis Outlaw's autograph," the kid shouted to the kite-fliers, stumbling away over the dunes.

Calyph shook his head. "That hurts me, damn."

"I'd have known it was you," I consoled him.

"You sweet."

"Sorry about the restaurant." I'd seen the place on a billboard, so it was my failure. "Are you hungry? I saw a fish market down the street."

"Kind of cheap of you to start being so thoughtful now."

"That's true," I allowed.

Keeping his face hard and unamused, he chuckled, like a cough. "So you're a good lackey when ain't no girls around? Have I got that right?"

I sucked in sea air, and felt the roots of my teeth tingle in the cold. I nodded humbly.

"Lucky I got no wife," he mused. "You ever have any urges to, like, do some weird shit to the serval or anything?"

I informed him I had no weird serval urges.

"You locked that boy in the closet one time. Didn't know if it was a fetish."

The memory of my doing that was such a fleeting part of a set of violent, confused images that for a moment I thought he was making it up. "I only have the usual fetishes," I said stiffly, and we sat a moment in what felt like harmony. Having to fire me had brought out his tenderness, and being on the way out I could say what I wanted.

"I'll put that in your references," he said.

"I'll never do this again," I said quietly.

"No? You could. You aight at it."

"I am?"

"Sure."

"I broke your leg," I said. "And your marriage. You ought to fire me faster before we see what else I can do."

As soon as these words left me I had a moment of awful foreboding, for slipping the truth by him like that so flippantly, for no purpose but my own pleasure. I suspected him of being smarter than me all the while, and it was a terrible risk to give up anything his paranoia might so easily light on. But then I watched him let my words go by, like so much empty boasting. He let them pass so easily I wondered if his innocence was as much a pose as mine.

"You know I don't fault you, Jess. You know I don't wanna end it here, either. But I vouched for you, to people whose respect I gotta have. Ain't nothin' to be said now. Shoulda found some other girl. We might be able to find something else for you when your time is up, is all I'm saying."

"If you aren't dead by then," I said, and I laughed through my teeth, and he through his, and together we watched the wind blow clots of foam out of the sea.

When we got back from the coast, the house was as dark as I ever saw it. Within the security gates there was no need to keep an illusion of habitation, and as we came around the last curve the front of the house loomed before us in the twilight like a place where nobody lived—an abandoned construction or a foreclosure.

When the car came to rest, the security lights clicked on, and I got out to retrieve the bags. Everything I did seemed to make a lot of noise. Calyph stood on his sticks, looking up at the dark windows with an unreadable expression.

"Told the fam I wasn't coming back till tomorrow," he explained at last, handing me a ring of keys. The use for each was written on it on tape, and I crunched the front door key into the lock.

As I carried the bags upstairs, Calyph swung into the living room, but when I got back he hadn't turned on any lights. He stood awkwardly looking out the window at the driveway, and the last weak traces of day just lit the edges of the suit of armor behind him.

"Let's go for a walk," he said.

He waved off a flashlight, and we circled around the edge of the house in the gloaming. The grill that had shone so blindingly that midsummer day was covered in canvas, but the outdoor court looked like it might have still been full of hidden children. We passed by the spot where I'd been berated and then given a sandwich, and I thought how long it had been since Calyph had worn his aviators to upbraid me. That joke wasn't funny any-more—it seemed the tic of a younger man.

Along toward the Japanese garden, we stopped on the path, and I saw that flowers grew at our feet in a rough half-moon of dirt. Most of them were dry and withered, but a few yet stood upright, bright yellow even in shadow. There was a tentative look to them somehow, like they'd been planted by a regular person and not a landscaper. They must have been Antonia's flowers.

Calyph tried to lower himself to look, but his braced knee could hardly bend, so he only hung there, half-swooned between the crutches.

"Getting late in the year I guess," he said at last.

As he stood meditating over her little half-withered garden, I heard the drone of an engine coming nearer. He straightened quickly, and the same unreadable expression came onto his face.

"We left the gate open," I said. "Should I—"

"I got it," he said, and as he swung himself quickly through

CHRIS LESLIE-HYNAN (138

the wet grass, I saw his face was lost in hope, and guessed the source of his strange mood at last. He'd hoped to come back to find her home.

I trailed him as the sound grew louder. As he went around the front corner of the house, the engine quit, and when I came around I saw a big red Avalanche sitting in the driveway like a giant toy. Calyph stopped short at the edge of the drive.

"'Sup, Greg," he called.

"Hi," said Oden, stepping down from the cab with a tin in his hand. His ancient child's face jutted forward eagerly. "I brought you some macaroons."

"That sweet."

"Mom made 'em. Haven't seen you round the way, so I thought I'd bring 'em by."

"It's lucky I'm here," Calyph said quietly.

"What?"

"I said it's lucky I'm here," he said, louder, and his voice went out among the trees.

Sometimes I'd have dreams of staying with them forever. Getting an omelet in the kitchen, or even caught in traffic on some blue fall day, I felt at peace with my devotion, and optimistic of its future. If I could just find something to do, some act that would restore me to the dignified position they'd so naïvely started me in. All it would take was one perfect stroke, to bind me to them more tightly than ever.

Other times I felt just as sure we weren't really friends at all, that he was having me on. It was a social experiment, watching my character bend under his influence; or maybe he'd just grown accustomed to the queer allegiances of white boys tired of their own skin, and had got to missing them in the married, professional life.

As the days drained away, the only acts that made sense were the selfless ones and the sabotage. I knew there was only one thing of any value within my power to recover for him, and I daydreamed great plots for getting Antonia back. I wrote elaborate formal letters, all unsent, and imagined the day when I would don my somber best and ring her bell and tell her simply, we need you, come home.

But at the same time, on the same day even, I'd get suspicious and want to terrorize him a little, just to see if I could get away with it. When he was asleep and there was no one around I'd whisper at him through the intercom. I put a shard of ceramic flooring in his eggs and then pointed it out before his fork could reach it. He'd given up his crutches—I was sad to see them go—and I liked to loosen the rubber end of his cane.

But mostly I spent my days on some of the most trivial errands of my tenure. All the afternoon and into the evening we'd go to one wholesome place after another. To his local knee doctor, to the rehab center and the practice facility. One day, as though inspired by all this self-maintenance, he made me get a pointless oil change.

"You only need it every five thousand, minimum," I said. It was one of those quick-change places and we were waiting in the queue.

"Ras says we should dump the oil, go synthetic."

"It's synthetic now."

"He say it's dirty. He tested it."

"He's just trying to discredit me." Although I didn't have the equipment to do the change, the pan and the wheeled board and whatall, during my first week on the job I'd bought the stuff myself to take to the shop. I'd done my research, found the part number for the filter, got the finest oil and the best price.

Now we rolled forward and I watched these men with

old-timey hats and mustaches eagerly undoing my work. One of them even had to pull out the air filter to show us how dirty it was.

"Yeah, yeah. Change that, too," Calyph said.

I turned on him. "It's supposed to look like that."

"Then it's your job to hide it from me," he said, shrugging.

"That'll be eighty-four ninety-five," a mustache told us.

"This is why Antoine Walker is bankrupt," I said as we pulled away.

"Motherfucker, drive."

"Pip, Spree, AI. You next," I said. "You think you can live off what that suit of armor get you, you got some surprises ahead."

The intimacy of getting cussed at had been the highlight of my day, and I thought we could take it a little further. I thought I'd wade in for once. He came back at me, and at first I didn't even really hear the words; I thought we were in for a good tussle, that I'd be able to hold my own. Then I started to process, and at the same time he seemed to lean forward into another gear of anger. When he got loud, his mouth seemed to move twice as fast. His contract still in doubt, money was probably the wrong subject. His anger flared and I realized I stood no shot, that I would be destroyed.

"I'm sorry," he said. "Did you start to talk different? Seem to me you did."

"Naw," I said, fatally.

"Naw! Yeah, seem to me you left your white voice off back there with those bow-tie men and now you wanna talk in *mine*."

"I hardly think . . ."

"You hardly do! I try to vouch for you the length of a week and damn if you don't jump that lisper in the tub. You try to transcend your hanger-on self, but you think that's how to do it. To get up in what's spoken for! You can't find your own white girl getting naked on the Internet and calling it art, in this town? That's some sorry shit, J.

"But you wanna talk about my expenses, so let's talk about why I keep you on with this thirty here. I need to keep you a few more weeks, see, under observation like. I figure in 'bout three weeks, you might just be the lightest-skinned brother I ever saw. One of these days it's gonna come *Black Like Me* up in this car, and no amount of green is gonna make me miss that fuckin' miracle."

I was quiet. I didn't think he knew about that book.

"So who next?"

"You are," I said softly. "You are the next."

Now that I only lived there on my days off, the bachelor's house was full of sad, warm light; it felt homey for the first time. Full of his own nostalgia for the place, the house cat followed me up to my narrow door.

From atop a stack of books on Native spirituality, the bachelor's ancient answering machine was blinking for the first time in months. I'd been asked to monitor his affairs in the lower forty-eight for emergencies, so I hit play and sat stripping off my socks, yellow with sweat and wood dust.

"Hello, Thomas, this is your mother," said a dry, querulous voice. "Please call home. I never know where you are or what you're doing anymore. Your father's getting holes in all his socks, but he won't let me take them, he says he doesn't notice. Something to remember for his birthday, which is the twenty-fourth. You know that, I'm just telling you. Wool socks are a nice gift, I don't care what anyone says. I'm worried about you, Thomas, so please call as soon as you can." A hoarse, strangled voice came roaring up inarticulately in the background and the message beeped off.

A picture of the bachelor's parents hung just above the machine, next to the watercolor nude. They both had big thatches of seventies hair, and it was hard to attach them to the voices in the message. I'd never heard someone so old talked to like they were so young. I was about to go for a clean shirt when my phone trembled and I saw I had my own message waiting.

"Hello, Jesse," said a tired voice. "Your grandmother's not well. Please call when you can. This is Rose." My aunt always left the brusquest messages. All the family knew it would be grandmother's time soon, that she might not be with us at Christmas, drinking brandy in her immobilized rocking chair. Hearing one message after the other, I felt a lack in my family's ways, an absence of color.

As I flipped the phone down, I saw that a text had been waiting, hidden behind the voice-mail prompt.

"Do you still work for me?" it read.

Portland opened on the road that year, Calyph's absence lost amid the hype of Oden putting up 14, 10, and 5 in his debut. Calyph hadn't traveled with the team, and after their three-game trip ended with a loss to the Rockets I drove him to a rap show.

"Come in and kick it awhile," he said. "I might need you."

I couldn't imagine what purpose I could serve. "Won't I need a ticket?"

He pulled two from an envelope and spread them with a little flourish, like they were hundred-dollar bills.

I wondered for what better company the extra had been meant. "Thanks," I said, and he made a sharp negating noise through his teeth, as though he were spitting out the negligible value of the gift.

Later, under the hype man's harangue, stiff white hands were being raised in the air and waved like they just did not care.

"He's just a rascal," the sampled soul singers cried as the beat kicked up. Behind the hype man a figure lurked in the murk at the back of the stage, shadowboxing in the unshadowed black. The wavering hands reached out to him.

"He's just a rascal," the sample cried. "Dizzee Rascal!"

With one more call from the hype man, the figure hopped forward into the light, wearing a silky gray hoodie, the unbent brim of his black-on-black Yankees hat skewed stage right.

"Oi!" he shouted boisterously. "G'won boi! G'won . . . Port-lan'!" And at this, Dylan Kwabena Mills, the Dizzee Rascal, looked out over the cluster of cloud-pale faces, the women with boyish haircuts, the men with effeminate ones, their hands raised limp as the drowned, and yielded to a brief fit of hysterical giggling. The hands fell down in relief.

I was glad to be at the bar, drinking root beer and enacting only the safe, familiar gestures of my awkward race. It felt good to be a white man who was not making a spectacle of himself. Over in the merch booth, two girls selling shirts that said "Buck the Blitz and Blamma" leaned on plump piles of hoodies with the confidence that they were not there for pleasure, and so need not be embarrassed, and I watched them watch Calyph.

He was alone on the far side of the room, and the light from the glowing log walls lit up half his face as though in gold leaf. We'd been sitting during the opening acts, and no one'd really noticed him, but now he stood tall and looked out upon the stage, projecting a tolerant repose against the slow accumulation of curiosity. In the absence of his crutches he looked freer and wilder, and I felt a certain relief at how thick his cane was, how much weight he had to put on it. He couldn't run off anyplace yet.

I felt my pocket vibrate with a single buzz. "Greyhound w Belvedere."

I tried to put the drink on Calyph's tab, and the bartender eyed me doubtfully. When I told him I was his chauffeur, he snickered and handed the glass over as though I'd earned it with a clever lie.

When I brought him the drink, I could feel the heads turning around me. Our hands met around the glass, his fingers in mine, and the room's curiosity was so palpable that for an instant I was sure I was bathed in light.

Later still, when the curious girls had come and gone, and given me cool conspiratorial looks, and Calyph thorny looks from the hothouse flowers of their eyes, and left us feeling entirely alone, we went upstairs to a table in the corner. So far that night I'd not come out from behind my uniform at all, and that seemed to make it easier for us to sit together and order two plates of biscuits and gravy and drink Hennessy and Sprite. We drank fast, and the second glass fell over us like the lens of a nostalgic film. We talked about being in college in the same year, when I was a senior and he a freshman, and I looked into the street expectantly, awaiting the women in skirts and bright letterman's sweaters who would twirl romantically along the sidewalk, kicking up rich clusters of leaves. I never went to college with anybody like that, but that's just how I remember the autumning of the old quadrangle.

Tipsy and restless, he was hot to talk, and suddenly his wife was an open subject again. I felt vaguely gratified to learn that Antonia had loved a woman before she loved Calyph, and when he tried to shy away from the details of his persuasion I wasn't about to let him.

"And then you . . . ." I said. "How did you?"

"Didn't do nothin', really. Think I wanted to be one more fool who thought he could turn her? I was kinda militant back then—think I even wanted to date a white girl?"

"So . . ." I said.

"You know, destiny and shit."

I stared him down, unsatisfied.

"I dunno. I felt it, but it was just like this distant overpoliteness between us at first. Then I started getting scouted, started seeing my name in the draft lists and thinking about jumping. I knew I'd be in some random city the next year, getting a house, a money manager, all that. College was winding up quick and all these other folks seemed like kids suddenly. Like amateurs at whatever they did, who didn't know just how green they were. Who might just go on with their playtime lives for years, just dabbling in this and that, like for them it wasn't gonna come to this adult shit too soon. Except A. Her family had expectations."

He tossed a big cube of ice into his mouth and chewed it violently. "I didn't turn her," he said finally. "I was just inevitable."

He started in on their courtship, full of sexual ambiguity and openhearted gestures and race hate and other meaningful things. I imagined what it might be like, to be high on some campus thick with rolling greens, towering and lithe; to be one at whom small women made rare with blue money, who smelled like summer for three whole seasons, and in the fourth maybe the leather of old libraries, sighed, and put aside what had only yesterday been desire, and said: All that, enough of that; this man, he is inevitable.

Well, I was inevitable too.

"I thought she might be going with a girl," I said, very by-the-by.

"What?"

"I'm sure she wasn't," I said quickly. "There was just this girl who came to your party. I saw them together a couple times, but before I could feel anything about it enough to tell you, it was over."

"What she look like?"

I tried to describe her, and watched his hands curl tight around the glass. I could feel my face go masklike in the presence of his suppressed emotion.

"I'm sure it wasn't anything," I repeated.

"That's the same girl," he said. "That's Frances."

I'd described her terribly, only really remembering her tattoo. "How can you be sure?"

"I'm sure," he said.

He looked so stern and righteous, it was easy to provoke him. It was wonderful to see someone so noble about love.

"So. You worried?" I asked.

I expected to see him rear up proudly. Instead he gave that short asthmatic laugh, and a defensive look came into his face. "Should I be?"

"I don't know."

"You ever see anything?"

"I never *saw* anything . . ."

"I can't be worried," he declared.

"You could," I corrected him.

Now he pulled up. He raised his chin and looked down at me, proud and faintly terrifying. His face had a stony, Old Testament quality—he was like some priest of love, frowning at a blasphemy I'd made against the purity of his position as a faithful and unwavering lover.

"Well, you had to wonder," I said, almost disdainfully. "After you found out about the house." I wasn't only goading him. I couldn't believe there wasn't some stage at which, even against his will, he gauged the legitimacy of the threat. He'd kicked her out alone into the whole world.

I could see the anger in his face advance and retreat. "Boy, whose wife is this?" he said, and then he looked away. "She knows she couldn't enjoy it," he said at last, and I felt my mind hurry in vain to see everything about Antonia new again in the light of this observation, this flare shot into the murk of his wife's mystery.

I left him at the table with his heavy soda and his pride and made for the bathroom. When I got back the food had come, and there was a guy in our booth getting his ticket stub autographed. He had on a stocking cap, and his face was angelic and slightly askew.

"Don't you eBay that shit," Calyph warned.

"You aren't worth anything," the guy said, beaming.

"Put it in a drawer, you'll see."

"My drawers are full," he said, leaning back like it was he who was the one getting approached by the random public. "I live in the moment."

He seemed to want a confidence contest, but my gravy was getting cool. He was sitting in front of my plate, and I put my shadow over him hoping he'd take the hint. Calyph looked at me and laughed and gave the guy a little backhand wave.

"I gotta move for this guy?" he asked.

"Yup."

"Thanks for the ink," he said, sliding out slowly. "I'll see you down the way."

When I sat, the booth felt too warm under me. "Who was that?"

Calyph shrugged and started going at his plate with a bottle of Mrs. Dash he'd pulled from somewhere. "Guy was like, 'Hey, you pitch?'"

"He thought you were MLB?"

Again he laughed.

I made some noise with which I pretended to understand. "Where'd you get that Dash?"

"Brought it," he said. "I knew we'd wanna eat." This was such a minor idiosyncrasy, I thought it must've come forward from his early days. I saw him at twelve, stepping off a bus in a waffle house parking lot with his AAU team, grasping the bottle of seasoning in his pocket with homesick satisfaction.

The kid was over at the bar, looking back at us like he had the wrong idea.

Calyph had taken off about half a biscuit in his first bite, and a bit of gravy was hanging in his beard. "Watch this," I said.

"What?"

Taking my napkin, I reached over and wiped his chin clean. It was just a quick swipe, but I was careful to get it all.

He gave me a slow sort of evaluative look that made me drop the napkin back to the table like evidence. "Thanks," he said, dry as my whitest friend.

I looked back to the bar. The guy was still staring, and for a second I held his gaze. I can't put to words what I was asserting. It was some kind of possessiveness, sure. I knew how it looked, to run this angel face off, to touch the man near his mouth with a soft napkin. I'd gone through a lot to sit at that table in a tenuous brotherhood that was at once disingenuous and the truest feeling I knew. You couldn't come in while I was away two minutes with a knit hat and some excessive body heat and take my place.

"Can I get that Dash?" I asked, and we ate in silence.

When we were through, I lifted my glass and through the ice I saw him, head bowed, turning his ring of simple gold like a cereal-box trinket. His eyes were shut, and they twitched a little behind the lids.

"Can't believe I forgot to take this shit off," he said.

"What?"

"You ain't heard anything from her, right? Nothing at all?"

"No." I didn't want to tell him about some little text. I wanted something substantial to give him, something impressive.

"What kind of baller am I, kick my wife out can't even fuck around?"

"You have a great love," I heard myself say.

He looked up at me wearily, so wearily. The declaration had probably seemed like a taunt, but I couldn't deny it, theirs was the greatest love I knew. He lived in a rarefied world where fealty was an almost embarrassing aberration, and she'd meant to leave him almost from the beginning, but still I trusted him and Antonia to live in a world of stronger and longer-lasting love than the world that was tangible to me, and I was going to persist in this faith, bound up as it was in what first drew me to them, until they let me down.

"You think she loves me? With that house?" he scoffed. "Half the team got some type of city place like that. They get the same man to put the pole and the ceiling mirrors in the bedroom. I know that house."

"I don't think there's any pole," I said, and I said it like I was sure.

"Oh, *you* been there?" His anger came and went like the pain of a falling iron, felt only after it passed. He was composing himself again before I knew what had happened. "'Course you have," he said, soothing himself. "'Course you have."

"I can tell you where."

"I saw that paper. I don't want to know any more," he said.

"It's just a bright little cottage-type—"

"Boy, I do not want to *know anything*." His eyes were on me, overwhelming, huge and choked and impossibly white.

I picked up my glass and put it down again. My fingers didn't look right holding the liquor. They looked like fingers for holding small glasses of bitter beer.

"You should take her back," I said. "That's all I'm saying."

"How could I?" It seemed only a blast of drunken pride, and

then he said, "Ask her old girl. Ask her family, everyone she ever know. Once you let A go, she gone."

"That can't be true. Not in this."

"One-way A!" he cried, and all of a sudden he was plainly drunk and his head was between his hands at the edge of the table. "Fuck, man. I came here to get one back on her. Why you think I'm here? With my ring on and a ticket for a girl I stood up 'cause I ain't want to say two words to her? I can't do it, J. You got to help me."

"Help you," I said softly. I looked at the bowed head between the wide, powerful shoulders in disbelief. All night, all those days I'd been waiting to be shown that he was not really as isolated as he seemed, that there was some community supporting him beside his teammates and his family. And yet here he was, resting his forehead now on the backs of his crossed wrists as though he might any moment go to sleep, doing an excellent impression of being just as much the brotherless loner as I.

"I got you," I said, and reached for my phone, and sent off the message to Antonia that had been waiting saved since the afternoon. "Always," it read. It'd seemed so plain, and I'd wanted to elaborate, but now it felt just right. Then I reached out my hand to touch him, to comfort him, and saw it stop. I wanted, as you know, to love him, to kill him, to be him. How do you touch someone with that in your hands?

"I got you," I said again, and cupped him a moment on the back of the head.

When we pulled up to the bachelor's house, he looked asleep. I had to jerk to a stop to rouse him.

"Where we at?" he asked, his tongue thicker than before.

"This is where I live," I said. "Come see."

He looked up at the dark house dully, and for an instant his fine, almost manicured eyebrows rose up. He must've thought I lived in some anonymous warren, a place with an antique buzzer system and a name like an old flophouse hotel. Then he leaned back again against the window and shut his eyes.

"I can't feel my face," he announced.

I let the belt slip, trying to think of a way to make him get up and go on with the night. I was lightly buzzed and full of energy, and he looked so shamelessly asleep.

And then I felt the urge to wake him in just the wrong way, just because. So I leaned over and tapped him. I'd heard of this tapping as a bro thing, a thing done among athletes and teen assholes. It made me glad I'd got out of high school before it was popularized. I never had the slightest thought of doing it to anyone else, and I think I did it wrong. I went forehand, like a slap or a harsh cupping, as if I were stripping a football from a quarterback. In hindsight, backhand was the way.

Still, he felt it.

His knees shot up, good and bad together. He didn't go fetal quite, but he was protecting his essence. He made a long *oh* sound. Then he took a nursing silence, wincing, gathering himself. When he looked at me again I didn't want to be in the car anymore.

I jumped out and ran up the steps a bit, laughing, feeling ridiculous and fine, as if through one sack tap I'd transformed myself into one of those mischievous figures from antiquity. I imagined myself with a rakish three-cornered hat.

"Boy, I will choke you out," he shouted through the painfully peaceful neighborhood. I glanced back and he was limping like five different ways.

On the porch I got the key out and the cat beneath the grandfather clock lifted its head angrily, like it was enforcing quiet hours. I could have kept him out if I really had to, but it was too simple just to bar him and be safe. I went up the narrow stair with this cacophony of wounded athletic struggle behind me, the cat running up between my legs.

I got to my door and it was cracked open. I thought I must have left it unlocked. I went up and there were too many lights on, and again I thought it my own oversight. I stopped a second in the kitchen and it was all quiet but for the off-kilter stomping beneath.

Then a man with white hair came out of the bedroom, my bedroom, wearing a string of dull beads around his neck, holding a book. We'd never met, and I'd not have recognized him but for the pencil sketch on the wall behind the television. In the sketch he was sitting in a garden, with an empty book and a pen on the table beside him, the expression on his face of such corny and exalted contemplation that I thought of it as his musing picture. Book or no book, the man before me didn't seem to be doing any musing. He looked angry and fearful and half-mad, and the sketch was a far better likeness than I'd imagined.

I felt Calyph come up the stairs and stop beside me. The presence of this oldster stilled us both.

"The fuck is this?" Calyph asked, breathing hard.

"I got kicked out," the man said. "I got kicked out of Alaska."

"You're the bachelor," I said.

"Bachelor nothin'! I'm just married." He turned to Calyph and his hoop earring glittered a little in the dull light. "I heard you got injured."

"Yes sir," he said. "Is this your house?"

"Of course it's my house. They run me off the reservation, you think I'm gonna come back where it's not my house?"

I stared at him a moment helplessly, this soft residue of old posters and silly ties turning into a force of nature in front of me. "I thought—"

"There's no thought to have. Whose beads are these? Whose life is on these walls? The walls know whose house it is up here."

"He rents," I interpreted.

"It's my life up here," he almost shouted. "But now I got to move. I been waiting for this all my life. I got a new native bride to prepare for. She can't live up here. This is where I lived when I was preparing for her. I've got to find someplace new to prepare for us together. So here's the deal. You two can stay here as long as you want. Inn-definite sublet. I just want my cut."

"He doesn't live here," I said. "He's got his own house."

"You think I don't know that? He's a god-damned professional basketball player! I can't believe I rented my house to a man who thinks on such a basic level."

"You got a great place here," Calyph said.

"Thank you," the bachelor said. "I hope you enjoy it. I'll be in and out of here, getting my valuables, but I'll clear out at night so you guys can do your thing."

There was a silence. The bachelor leaned back on his heels contentedly. He understood everything; he had defined everything. I looked at Calyph uncomfortably, almost forgetting to check if he still wanted to give me a beating.

"He's got a wife, too," I said.

"I'm sure he does. Every player needs a wife. How else are you going to get any love in your life, just going city to city fucking everything nice? You do it that way, you only learn how to love other men. *Philía*, I mean, the brotherly love. Excuse me."

"I lost her," Calyph said. "I sent her away."

"What'd she do?" the bachelor demanded. I don't think I'd ever heard anyone ask him so plainly.

"She bought a house. She bought another house and she didn't tell me."

The bachelor chuckled for a long, slow time, and it was the only sound. "You kids!" he said. "All those vows and that's what it takes? My wife tried to run off with a bootleg pilot two days after the wedding, and tomorrow I'll be picking out curtains. Don't get me wrong. All lives are different. You're a public figure, I can't presume to know. But you've got to have some faith, Mr. West. Faith is what takes you from that kind of pride that says you have to send her away to that kind of pride that lets you let her come back."

"Your mom called the other day," I said. I felt Calyph must be fed up at this speechifying man and his book-sale wisdom. I'd rather have been wrestled to the ground than to stand there silent any longer before that reedy ersatz oracle.

"Nah," Calyph said. "You right. You exactly right."

"I know it," the bachelor said. "I know it and you know it. We've been through things. Different things, but things. This kid, I don't know, he can't even keep my plants alive."

"Your father's birthday is the twenty-fourth," I said dully. "Your mom was thinking socks. Your fucking plants are fine."

"Fine! This kid couldn't keep a stick alive. He couldn't grow popcorn." He looked at me sharply. "You been jackin' off in the shower," he said. "I can tell."

Calyph began to laugh uncontrollably. It started as just air going in and out, but soon his whole frame, which that night should have been in Texas setting picks on Tracy McGrady, was shaking wildly, his voice cracking like a teenager's.

"Maybe if you jacked off on those plants they'd have some nourishment and we wouldn't have a problem," the bachelor said. Calyph just got worse; his shrieking laughs filled the whole attic. The bachelor looked on proudly, like someone had laid the scepter of the king of comedy in his age-spotted hand.

He took Calyph by the shoulder. "Come see my library," he

said. "You might borrow one or two things." Calyph went with him, without so much as a look at me, and there were tears of laughter streaming out his eyes, and they left me there, in the kitchen, which felt then like a dreary antechamber where boys with small, dry hearts who knew nothing must sit and wait until they are needed again, for any trivial purpose at all.

8

The next morning I woke to the sound of the bachelor pouring condiments down the sink. If the place had ever been mine in any sense, it had been mine in sound, the sound of silence when I wanted it, and when I came out of the bedroom to see him thumping a bottle of cocktail sauce and listening to his Mayan jams on a dusty boom box, I knew I'd be spending my day off somewhere else.

I was walking downtown through the lunch-hour crowd when I saw the old Pontiac. Parked with the top down among a row of Civics and Hyundais, it didn't look out of place so much as it imposed its own style on the block. The license plate read "PH4R40," and it transformed a whole length of Alder into a street scene from a seventies film in which all the modern cars were only so many errors of continuity. The driver's seat was empty, but Goat was riding shotgun. His hair had grown out a little, and his fragile outpatient look had swelled into health. He looked stronger and even less sensible than before. I was on course to pass right by him, and before I'd decided whether to duck away he put his hand up, and I felt the unpleasant suction of greeting an outgoing person of theoretical importance whom one dislikes.

"Jess," he said, grasping my unoffered hand. "I'm back in!"

"What?"

"Toronto signed me. Moon's out for the year," he said.

"Congratulations," I said. "Why are you here?"

"Toronto's in town. I'm suiting up tomorrow."

"What happened to Moon?"

"Someone shot him in the leg or something," he said. "Terrible."

"Terrible," I repeated.

"I love Canada, man. I can't wait. They're weak at the three, and I should get some better overseas offers now."

"Where've you been since the coast?" I was surprised to find him with the Pharaoh. Savier had seemed to despise him even before the night he'd attempted every available wrong, and I couldn't see their having any lasting relation.

"I hung around awhile," he said vaguely. "Went up and down the coast looking at some beaches. Had a tryout in L.A. I was on my way back north to run a camp in Coeur d'Alene when I got the call. Right off I called up Savier. I wanted to make things right with him."

"Sure."

"You should make things right, too," he said, in this earnest let's-all-take-the-straight-road kind of voice.

"I was just bathing," I said.

"Right!" he laughed. "Well, all's fair. They're engaged now, did you hear? He asked her the day we left. I'd want Odette locked down, too, after that."

"Sure," I repeated vaguely, half disbelieving him.

"Savier's going to hook me up with a good staff once I get signed and settled," he hurried on. "We're starting small, but I owe him that. He knows how to do it, right? Maybe he could help you find another position."

"I got a position," I said.

Again he laughed carelessly, and scratched at the growth of stubble on his cheek. It was as though having a job again had stripped him of any of his remaining likable vulnerabilities. "Hell, cut him out of it, right? You and me, Jess. Canada! Who knows? I'm serious, I could use you. Think it over."

He dipped into his pocket and I thought he was going to dole out a freshly dried business card that said "Lucas Montaigne, SF, Toronto Raptors." Instead he handed me two tickets to the game. In that mood, he'd have given them out to the men on the corner drumming on caulk buckets—every open gesture he could make reinforced his own triumphant return.

I thanked him and told him I'd think it over, and then I got on. The Pharaoh had taken his anger out on me in the briefest and least demeaning way possible—he had punched me almost without breaking stride, and I doubted I was worthy of a second scene. All the same, I didn't linger. To remain with Goat was to despise him for the man he was, and myself for tolerating him. Behind it all lay the memory of Shida, and the one part of that evening when my misbehavior was not in some sense a success. At the end of the block I turned back and found myself wishing to see the Pharaoh, to see someone with a code to judge me by, but there was only Montaigne, dangling his legs over the door.

I had to be in by seven-thirty the morning after. Going down Macadam, a fat kid in a white headband ran across the median wearing an old Randolph jersey, and I thought again of all the rest of the team, spread out around the city in the bleary morning light. I'd always hated the athletes I knew, until I met Calyph. In high school, when the world's full of them, they're the worst sort. The small, angry men coaching them, hoarsely shouting, presiding over their buzz-cut dictatorship, giving facile, self-serving lectures on what it means to be men; the pimply boys harnessed and made to run suicides; the hazing and the bullying. That was sport as I'd known it, sport like the lowest rung of some runt military, a humiliating way of getting fit and aligned into cannon fodder, as a substitute for anybody doing anything strategic or sophisticated.

But with the pros, you feel different—and you hear everything about the pros. Their grades have always been fixed, they name their children after themselves and then squander their inheritance. They go to clubs in every city after the games and take special rooms. You hear how they come home to their girlfriends and get into fights, drag somebody down a flight of stairs. But Calyph wasn't a bit like that. He had such an attitude of moral uprightness it gave me a pain. If he ever hit a woman in rage, it must've been because the pitch of their argument had risen so high that to make a hole in the wall behind her would've been just a cheap show and a diversion.

I drove up to the gates and put in the passcode, which remained unchanged with the new order. As the gate-halves pulled apart, the mist that clung to them ran off into rivulets. Approaching the house, the Mazda moved from the blacktop onto the gravel, and where I once heard that timeless hushing it now sounded like someone was viciously shaking a coffee can full of rocks beneath the car.

I put the car in the garage and took the Jaguar out and waited by the passenger door. It was just seven-thirty. I wondered where we would go today.

Looking up at the house, I saw motion from an upper window, as if a curtain had been brushed aside. In another moment I heard the noise of a motor behind me. It was a cab, not one of the suburban companies but a regular city cab. It came around the circle, crunching the stone, and pulled up on the far side of me. I looked for a passenger, but there was only a peaceful-looking Middle Eastern man behind the glass, staring straight ahead with a bored smile.

I stepped toward him and he rolled down the window a little, the smell of leather and the city leaking out.

"Who're you here for?"

He consulted the cab's ancient electronics. "Ramses," he said in a distinct voice.

"He's not here," I said.

"Okay, man, but they buzz me in."

"He's not here," I said again.

He smiled at me, shrugging helplessly, and then I heard the front door open.

"That's for me," a woman's voice lisped.

She stood on the top step, frowning beneath a pair of over-large sunglasses. I had the idea she didn't want to give up the high ground. She wore a simple black tee and a pair of green sweatpants, as though she might just now be embarking on a run, but for a pair of canvas slippers. Her "broken" finger was all healed, and a large rectangular bandage now protruded from beneath her sleeve.

"Ramses," the cabbie said serenely.

At the sound of what might still have been her future name, Odette skipped quickly down the steps. I remember looking down, marking the progress of her tiny plump toes half-protruding from the slipped-on shoes.

"I don't propose to speak with you," she said.

I glanced up and she was blushing as she went by. I turned to the cab, meaning to direct something demeaning about her to the driver, but could think of nothing sufficiently cruel. The glass had gone up again.

"Congratulations on your engagement," I murmured.

"My what?" she cried angrily, yanking open the door of the cab.

I let her go and walked toward the house. All my limbs felt heavy. My head was light as an empty rind.

There was a single light on up the stairs, but the first floor was all dim. In the early sun it seemed almost cloudy inside—I got the feeling of wandering through slightly misty rooms. I wanted to go right up and confront him, to denounce him impressively, but I wasn't sure how to start. I wasn't the confrontational sort; I was afraid I'd be no good. I could see myself inarticulately aping the tense atmosphere of a bad film, a figure of no consequence, being turned lightly aside.

Instead I wandered through the rooms. I went to the cold hearth and looked in at the ashes. I picked up the poker and carried it around with me—it was soothing to hold something iron. In the hallway I looked at his Ninth Ward picture of the men on the stoop of the ruined house. It seemed a sort of pose now, to have that, to claim that special rage. Not all black guys got to be from New Orleans. I hadn't heard about his going down and helping. None of his were among the abandoned. I spat upon the picture and watched my thin spittle run down the gloss.

I wandered on to the living room and the suit of armor. I'd spent some idle time wondering about the period of the suit—it wasn't the heavy plate of classic knight armor, but it wasn't some light Bantu stuff, either. The torso was black, with a sort of supple Samurai look, the arms and legs of silver scale. A disc shield sat at its base, next to a freestanding spear with an intricate, curved tip. I touched the spear with the poker and then threw the poker aside. It fell to the carpet soundlessly.

The spear was an awkward thing, standing up to my shoulder. It seemed too heavy to throw but too light to do much else with. Using it like a walking stick, I paced across the room and came once more to the base of the stairs. I stood there a long moment, trying to gather myself, my mind empty, clutching at last the emptiness itself, and then I lifted the spear and jabbed hard with the butt at the wooden ball at the banister's end. It popped off cleanly and clattered down the hall. I looked up at the stairs, at all the white carpet between him and me, and felt my legs swollen with the heavy feeling of a coming cramp.

The bedroom door was open and he was lying on the bed. His back was to me, the twisted sheets wrapped tight around him from neck to toe. He was still. I walked to the foot of the bed, but I had a fear of going all the way, of seeing his face, in case he wasn't asleep but only tensed, waiting for me, his staring eyes gleaming out at nothing. I prodded him softly on the foot with the butt of the spear.

He writhed a little and moaned a distant complaint from within his sleep. I saw the muscle of his shoulder and the curiously skimpy hair of his armpit. He propped a new pillow over his eyes and curled in on himself like a protesting child.

I prodded him a second time and got no response. I swung the spear around.

I didn't poke him, it was just a tap, but he sat right up at last. In one motion both pillows were behind him and he was sitting up in bed as if prepared to take a coffee. His chest was hairless like a boy's.

He blinked at me. He seemed to be considering a serious but distant problem. "We got a beef here?" he asked finally.

"Yes," I said.

He nodded, eyeing the spear-tip slowly, as if to let me know he was taking it in, and though he trusted me fully and bore no suspicions of my having anything but the best intentions, it was being accounted for as a weapon.

"Get up," I said. "You're late for your appointment."

"What's the time?"

"Get up."

"You wanna toss me them clothes then?" I saw some folded stuff on a chair in the corner.

"You can dress yourself," I said.

He shrugged, and then I saw his arms flex and he hauled himself out of bed all at once, in a rush, making a strong gesture of it. He was all naked. I didn't want to see that, not at all. He was small and shrunken, but the way he stood, his hips directed toward me, it was like he figured I was motivated by some fetish. I saw myself as a petty torturer, making men show themselves to me, and felt the spear go loose in my hand.

"The sheet," I said, too loudly. He took his time dragging it loose. At last he wrapped himself and limped to the clothes. He picked them up in one hand, holding the sheet to his stomach, and then he paused.

"I'm not sure how we do this," he said. "Unless you wanna see some more." He cracked a punishing, too-comfortable smile.

"I'll turn around," I heard myself say.

He looked at me silently; the idea seemed to have thrown him. Although the spear was just something I happened to have, a kind of benign suggestion, I thought he must've still had some idea of disarming me. I stood in the corner of the room with my face to the wall and dared him to. I figured it was against his code, if my back was turned—and soon he was dressed. I turned back and he was wearing a T-shirt and track pants.

"Not like that," I said. "You want something nice for today, sir."

"It's just a checkup on the . . ." But he left himself unfinished.

"You never know where we might go," I said brightly. "A well-dressed man is prepared for anything."

Reluctantly he stripped down to his boxers. Once again I turned my face away, and although my nerves were near paralysis in confusion and dread, I whistled a happy tune. At last we stood in front of his closet, the master and valet, and chose him an outfit for the day.

His closet was a good one, and deep. I was surprised at its neatness and arrangement. Everything hung in rows from dark to light, and the swath of blacks separated solid and striped.

Only the shoes were haphazard, covering the floor unpaired and upended, like a harbor full of boating accidents. His suits were mostly all business: they agreed with the team's faceless aesthetic, but seemed to be held together by a classical sensibility. There were shoehorns and a collection of pocket handkerchiefs. There was a suit the color of honey butter that I imagined being worn poolside at a British country estate, while women in austere swimsuits came lightly across the lawn, nonplussing the butler by carrying their own towels. He saw me looking and reached for it.

"Not that," I said. "Where's your draft suit?"

I started leafing through the back row, looking for some kind of loud embarrassment. I figured his racks would hold at least a couple suits like the ones you see on draft night, the garish payday eyesores the more flamboyant lottery picks wear, in turquoise or cherry red, celebratory and regrettable as so many neon cocktails.

"This here," he said. He pulled out a light-gray suit so conservative it looked like some ticker tape might slip out of the pocket. I imagined Antonia's father nodding in approval and offering Calyph his first Rolex as a reward for not embarrassing his future family on television.

"Very nice," I said. "But let's find something the ladies might like a bit more. You never know when a nice juicy, loose one might go by."

At the very end of the row was a white suit with pinstripes of faint silver. I pulled on one of its sleeves approvingly.

"That don't fit me no more," he said, his jaw clenching around the words.

I said I thought we could give it a try.

The suit didn't seem so tight on him, but he struggled with it, and I wondered if he wasn't playing up his injury a little as he pulled on the snow-bright pants. "Where's your white hat?" I asked as I watched him buckle laboriously.

At last he stood before the mirror in the crisp suit of the pimp. His face was haggard with the morning, and a little seed of sleep still notched his eye. I came up and brushed one of his lapels to give him some confidence. "Very nice," I said, handing him his cane. "A real lady's man."

His suffering eyes watched me in the mirror. "Where to now?"

"I want to show you my room," I said. He'd still never seen it, and I wondered if he knew what a cell it was, how degrading.

"Sure," he said, in a tired, beaten voice. "But hey. We don't need that thing. We can just go like we are."

"What thing?" I asked brightly, letting the spear dip a little in my hand.

"That weapon you holding on me," he said. "If that's what you're doing."

I jerked the spear up defensively. I didn't want to acknowledge it was a real iron thing held against him. It was only a sort of emblem, of his sins against his faith and his code. While I held it, I'd have the power. It was simple. Holding it, I could show him what he'd done very clearly and simply, like I couldn't in words.

"It's not like that at all," I said.

"No?" His voice seemed to grow a little stronger, now that the spear had been spoken of.

"I'm just holding it," I said.

"It's pointed at me," he said, in a stronger voice still, tinged with mock confusion.

I almost told him that it wasn't, that it wasn't pointing at him or wasn't a spear at all, but I could hear how it would sound, the absurdity, and how it would feel to plead for him to obey me without mentioning the instrument of his subservience.

"It's meant for throwing," he said. "You ever throw a spear?"

"In a play."

"A real one?"

"I made it real."

"Yeah? Well you want to heave this one? Let it fly off the balcony maybe?"

"Maybe later," I said. My voice was shaking a little.

"You don't gotta hold that on me, Jess," he said, looking me in the eyes now, with his infuriating face, that summoned dignity easily even in disgrace. "I get what you think I done. I get why you mad. You don't need a spear to show me. Let's just give it a toss and then, what the fuck, we'll talk about it. Okay?"

I tried to stay wary, but his voice lulled me. I could feel my command and my invention falling away, and it seemed now that he was giving me an out. This toss was almost the only way I could think of now to get the spear away from me, to edge back into some kind of regular life. We turned to the sliding door beyond the half-shut curtain.

"After you," I said, and he drew open the door easily and limped out ahead of me onto the balcony. The sound of birds came at me through the morning wet, their cries like the far-off turn of a winch.

As I stepped to the door, I saw it all unfolding. I saw him standing aside, arms spread wide, convincing me of his passivity and benevolence. I saw him telling me how to throw the spear, coaxing it onto my shoulder. I saw myself standing in the doorway, backing up partway into the room to get a full stride—even measuring out the steps on a practice heave. I felt the spear in my hand, flopping heavily at its ends, and knew how pitiful this great warrior heave would be. But I saw myself imprisoned by this fate, and by his coaxing, unavoidably. I saw myself already striding forward, pivoting into the heave with my sad, stringy arms. I saw the spear release and dive, and heard it clang down pathetically on the patio below.

Before the sound had died away he'd be on me. I could hear his curses and feel myself go under. I could taste his black fists on me. He could probably lift and hurl me off the balcony easily enough—I'd sail as far as the spear. And all the while he'd be talking. I imagined him telling me how it was with Odette, to infuriate me, or defending himself with righteousness and great skill, so even as I was being beaten I would begin to regret my hasty judgment, to feel that his code remained unbroken, his noble faith unsquandered. As the blood filled my mouth I would come to see how right he was to take Odette in, to prove to himself how much he loved his own wife. Of course it'd been that way, I'd decide; it made sense now. I'd hear it all, and wish yet again to switch places with him, and I'd think of how even this, the thrashing of a small man who'd stepped beyond himself, would just be a savage little blip in his life, and then I would think of my own shriveled, duplicitous existence scrolling automatically forward without reward or meaning.

So, even though it was a small and pathetic thing, next to this culmination, I just locked him out there. He heard the sound of the door in its runner and turned and tried to get himself in the gap, but his knee failed him and he fell heavily against the pane. His hands flashed out and scrabbled against the glass, but I shut the door and clicked the lock in place.

I knelt to where he was, and we looked at one another through the glass.

"You shouldn't have done that," I said.

His face broke open a little then, into helplessness and pleading, and there wasn't any nobility anymore, just youth and fatigue and the premonition of his lasting discomfort. For an instant I felt I'd won, that I'd found myself an out in a last flash of intuition, but I knew it wouldn't last, that in another second all I would find to wish for was that it'd been someone else who'd imprisoned him, so I could be the blameless one, to come and rescue him, and get his thanks.

(9)

Driving back to town, I was sure helicopters would descend at any moment and beat the air above me into sound. I waited for the megaphone blast, the distorted voice from the heavens and its orders. I thought about how I'd always had an affinity for Canada and hoped to spend more time there. I thought of big empty Nunavut, of whether there were outlaw communities on Hudson Bay, of the beauty of Vancouver and what a shame it was they had to draft Steve Francis and Big Country Reeves and fail until they turned into Memphis. But I'd like it there, as I liked all places where the cold discouraged people from achieving anything for large parts of the year. Goat wouldn't be some towering figure in my life. Driving for him in Toronto would be like driving for some young fop who'd once had a hit song on the radio. I'd buy him car wax and mustache wax, and adopt all his lesser vices for my own, for the sake of companionship, and in hopes of someday despising his greater ones less.

After that, there could even be Europe. I saw the crumbling stone of some old seat of culture, the violet hour in a Belgian village, and the lights of cafés glistening on the water in Greece. For a moment it seemed like a tour that could go on almost endlessly, as inexhaustible as Goat's gradual decline through worse and worse leagues and my own capacity for reinvention. And then I reached the city I lived in, and realized I didn't know which exit to take, to get to where I ought to decide to be going.

I'd taken the Mazda, to show I wasn't going rogue or anything.

I blew north along the east bank, postponing my decision, thinking I might lose myself awhile on Hayden Island, or in the anonymous Couve. But coming up to Broadway, I saw the signs for event parking and pulled onto the ramp.

At the entrance to the makeshift lot, the yawning attendant looked at me strangely. "Game ain't till five! We just stakin' out now."

"Can I park all day?"

"I guess," he said, but his laugh was like a cackle at something people had never stooped to doing, and I reversed and drove on.

From Broadway it was an easy trip northward, past the barred shops advertising phone cards to the gleaming new blocks of Alberta. Stopped at a long light, I sent Antonia a message about the game. She'd been hinting at wanting to meet up, and while it seemed an odd venue for a talk, what with the cheering and the children, the spilled concessions, I did have the tickets; they were a valuable commodity. She didn't get back to me, though—she was always quick or not at all, and again the day stretched out ahead of me, aimless, perilous, and much too long. I was so near her neighborhood already, I thought I could park just a minute and take a look.

I'd expected her house to be bursting with life, with flowers and odd metal sculptures and the sharp smells of new herbs. Yet it wasn't much changed. She'd painted the porch rails a more muted color, but the place still had a spare look. The porch was empty save a thick welcome mat and a table with a single chair, and though the shades were up I could see no plants or decorations—no life, nor anything to suggest it. Her scooter was gone, and I sat ten minutes and saw no movement. I rolled down the window and a set of wind chimes tolled softly in the absence of human voices.

I got out and strode up to the porch with my head down and

knocked before I could unnerve myself. Without waiting for a reply, I went around the side of the house where I couldn't be spied from any window. No one came to the door.

There was a handsome wooden fence in back, too high to see over, enclosing the small yard. Twice I tried to scrabble over, but each time fell back defeated. I walked round to the other side of the house, and there let myself in by the open gate.

The yard was barren, just weak old grass and a small, unimproved concrete patio. Three bags of soil lay neatly stacked next to a bright tin can holding a few cigarette butts. I tried the sliding door, telling myself I only wanted to know if it was locked. It opened without a sound. I stood a moment on the threshold, letting the stale house air seep outward.

I don't claim to know all the ways people live when they live alone, but even if I've learned nothing from loneliness, I can at least identify it with the expertise of long experience, and as I walked through the small, sparse rooms, I knew that whatever it meant for Antonia to buy that house, and for Calyph to make her go live in it, she was deeply alone there. Our fear that she had another fell away a little more with each new room: the kitchen with its counter strewn with takeout menus and shelves of still-packed boxes; the hallway, empty of all decoration save for some dusty rubber mice kicked up against the wall; the tiny, dark bathroom, where a value-sized box of tampons sat open beneath the sink like an oblique feminist gesture.

In the living room I sat in an antebellum rocking chair and stared at one of the few accumulations of life in the house. It was her record player, and she'd bought every album I'd recommended to her and more—even the early releases I'd never managed much interest in. I put on something in a sleeve with an empty blue highway and went and cracked the bedroom door.

The room was a mess. A kerchief hung askew from an ugly

ceiling fixture like it'd given up trying to do anything about it. A cereal bowl sat on the nightstand, giving off the sweet smell of stale grain. There were little socks everyplace. I'd cleared off a spot on the bed and was considering a nap when I felt the strangeness of how much space I had. The bed took up most of the room; I stretched out my arms in both directions and met no edges. Putting my hand beneath the spread, I felt the extremely fine sheets. I felt myself lying over the hollow her body would make, obscuring it, blotting out the faint traces of the tiny curl of her limbs in the soft immensity. I got up and took a step back and studied the bed anew. Without any thought in my head, I brought out my phone and took a grainy and uneven picture of the thing. This was not a bed for lying alone, nor even for lying with another of normal size—the caption would read *second home*. I was trying to send it to myself when I heard a soft jangling noise, and then a bounding shape appeared from nowhere and with a triumphant hork the serval bit me on the thigh.

In the Rose Garden, Calyph was everywhere. I turned down the program and the stat sheet only to see his face beaming out from the wall along the escalator, airbrushed of every complicated emotion. In the gift shops you could buy a little stuffed bear wearing his number at a discount price. I saw a Native kid with beaded, braided hair wearing his jersey and wanted to run after him and ask if he knew what number eight had done.

It was my first live ticket in years, and the game felt unreal. Tiny in the wide arena, the players looked somehow semiprofessional. They all ran so fluidly, but their moves seemed basic and unremarkable, and even when Oden took a rebound and threw it down so the stanchion shook, it looked like there must be a hundred other guys from Indiana who could do it just as well.

I looked for Goat and he wasn't there. There was a lanky guy stretching in warm-ups in the corner off the end of the bench, obscured by the third-string center. I could just see his bony wrists when he touched his toes. For a quarter I assumed it was Lucas, like he was so new they couldn't find a chair for him, but then he got up and jogged back to the locker room and it was just an injured Spaniard everyone knew was headed back to Europe.

For the first time in days I felt the pocket buzz. "Already here," the phone said.

I stood and excused myself into the nachos of the family next to me.

"Quarter just started," the husband complained.

On the concourse I went for a binocular kiosk. The woman was pulling the vendor's umbrella out of its stand but her wares were still displayed.

"We're all out of 'Better,' " she said.

There was a "Good" for twenty that looked like a toy and a "Best" so bulky and complicated it must have had real scientific value, for fifty-five. Going back to my seat, I felt like I had a microscope around my neck.

"Nice specs," the man of the house said.

"Hey, mister, whose cheese is this?" his son asked, pointing down at their food. His mother smiled in silent pride. In her lap she held a handmade sign: ODEN FOR MVP.

Being in an open place brought back my paranoia, and all game I watched the screen whenever they showed crowd signs, prepared to drop something and look for it if they showed her.

Even with the binoculars, it took me until the fourth to find Antonia. She was in a private box, and until the game grew close she must have been behind glass, doing whatever they did there—sitting on a leather couch, eating rarefied appetizers, and drinking cocktails shaken with ice. From out of the blur I caught her leaning over the rail. She'd cut her hair short, and when I adjusted the one useful knob I could even see the fuzz at the back of her neck. She stood with her face turned away, but I knew—no one I'd seen all game looked so aloof in an arena. I saw her fragile-looking wrists as her hands grasped the rail, and her attentive chin, and I wondered what she saw, how much of the game she'd ever wanted to learn. She might've seen the pattern of it all, the lob coming before the pin-down was set, or it might've all been sweat and noise, a dull pageant of exertion she'd long treated as something to escape from.

"I see you," I texted.

"Meet at 216 entrance. I'll come down."

By the four-minute mark, our lead had stretched to fifteen. With the game in hand, I looked into the box in time to see Goat come out with two drinks and hand one to Antonia. I focused the lenses until the stubble on his smiling jaw leapt out.

"This guy's got ants in his pants," the cheese boy said solemnly as I scraped past his dad's khaki knees.

Coming down from the cheap seats, I circled the concourse until I found the number. There was a narrow red stair there that led up to the box level, carpeted to suggest opulence and guarded by a bald guy with a velvet cordon.

"Box ticket holders only, sir," he said in a worn-down voice.

"Why's it velvet?" I asked. "I never got that."

"Excuse me?"

"The rope. Why's it made out of that?"

I bumped up against his rope a little, to illustrate, like I was some kind of poor little boat drifting around, and the rope was helpfully redirecting me away from the rich boats and back into the main channel. I guess I was light-headed, but I really thought he'd understand.

He put his hand up then. He put it right under my chin and made contact. He pushed me back a little ways.

"Please step away from the rope, sir," he said. "There's no loitering here."

I gathered myself. I could feel myself brushing my shirt front and going up on my toes like some affronted fop.

"I'm waiting for my employer," I said.

It felt a long time since I'd adopted the proper servant manner. It came out stiff, and of course he didn't believe me. He stared at me with his beef-rimmed, unfeeling eyes, and then he reached for the two-way on his belt.

"Security," he said.

"You're security," I told him.

Just then I saw her little shoes coming down the stairs. She stopped with her hand on the rail. "That's her," I told him disgustedly.

The security man's belt jingled importantly as he turned to her.

"Can he come up?" Antonia asked.

"This man works for you, ma'am?" He didn't even have the decency to sound incredulous.

"Very hard," she said.

The man's neck wrinkled and the cordon lifted grudgingly away. I wanted to give him a stare, to put my hands up as I slid by him, but she was there. I had to be reasonable again.

And then I slowed, under her long-lost gaze. I felt like some albatross of hard science was hanging around my neck, and my thigh throbbed suddenly where her cat had bit me. "I brought you these binoculars," I said.

"Thanks so much," she said faintly. She was familiar as a sister after so long away. Her hair was mussed a little, and it was like something I'd been around all my life, like it'd gotten in my face when we'd slept together in our narrow summer beds. Whatever trouble and tension we'd had seemed a chance mistake. Even that night with the sheets felt like just some minor role-play, devoid of permanent consequence. We knew each other, we mostly got along, and here we were again, in this stairwell of thin, unconvincing luxury. In my brief life of service, her wary face and inscrutable jokes were some of the oldest living things.

She put out her cool hand, and when we shook it felt listless and rote. I sensed she was in a bad way, but could only guess at how she'd stand up to the latest, worst news. I couldn't decide whether I wanted to tell her about Odette, whether it would spark the fight that would bring her back to him or turn her further away into the furtive dwindle of her new life.

"I didn't know you went to games," she said as we went up along the inner hall, hung with old framed jerseys.

"I didn't know you did."

"Lucas insisted."

"You know him?"

"From his stint here last year. I kind of liked his old girl. I guess she's gone now."

"We were at the Pharaoh's together."

Her pace slowed just slightly. "I'd always hear about that place. Did you go cliff diving?"

"I wasn't that kind of guest."

She asked about my work and I put on a faraway smile, as though in reminiscence of the nice quiet time Calyph and I were having together. I found myself wishing she would ask after him. Had his brother come and found him yet? It was his day off, so it wasn't certain—he might still be huddled there, shivering, his white suit growing heavy with dew. I wanted to tell her all of it, to confess and compel her return—and then Goat's face appeared down the hall.

"We await you," I said. I tried to say these strange words clearly, without any slant, and then he was on us. He took us both by an arm and led us inside, the self-congratulatory good cheer coming off him in waves. His smile was large and fixed—he dared us not to like him as though it were a dare at all. There was a wet spot on his jacket that smelled faintly of tonic.

"A great day," he kept saying. "A great day."

"Why didn't you play?" I asked.

"I wasn't gonna get any minutes tonight. Why play when you got a box? We got this box as long as we want it, people!"

"Just till nine," laughed the attendant. I could hear the public-address announcer doing his postgame wrap through the glass.

A half ring of cushion-backed stools had been pulled around opposite a black leather couch, where Goat sat center. There was some X Games–looking guy on his left, and on his right he'd left room for Antonia. The table in the center was a mess of sad and basic snacks in gleaming glass bowls.

The rest of the crowd was split between those trying to look like the money and those trying to look like the talent. Some were older, in business clothes, and they ranged up in age far enough that I wouldn't have been surprised to see Goat's parents there, huddling proudly. The rest were familiar counterculture—there was even a white girl who made blond dreadlocks look acceptable. She ushered Antonia over next to Goat and made her drink something fizzing with a lime in it, and as she settled in the room's open gaiety felt suddenly forced.

All I remember of our time in the box was Goat's advance. I never can believe in people who have love for everyone, but his main problem was his love always coming back to Antonia. "Sweet times are here again," he'd say in a singsong voice, and she'd nod back doubtfully. He sprang up from the couch in order to get her a glass of water and six people had to move out of his way. He touched her knee relating an unfunny story, and when she laughed politely back at him I resented his draining her social energy.

Abruptly he turned to me. "I'm back in the palace," he said, in a voice taken by its own myth-making.

If there was anything sympathetic to find in him anymore, it was there in his desperation to let everyone know he could roll high once more. It was clear he knew how tenuous it all was. A little of that old hospital fragility clung to him in his forced happiness, and you could see he sensed how rarely the horn sounded for the twelfth man, how often they sat there waiting to be evaluated solely on the enthusiasm of their cheering, vying only for the team spirit award, until they were sent away again, to some obscure hinterland.

The Cali punk next to him laughed into his sleeve tattoo. "Some palace," he said.

"This place should have a Jacuzzi," said the dreadlocked girl.

"Look at it," Goat said, insisting at the emptying arena with a thick-jointed finger. "That's the most famous building in the city right there. Blimps fly over it. The whole country knows Portland from this place."

"I used to like to stay in and watch the games," Antonia said suddenly. "If it was a national broadcast, they'd always show the river and the bridges and the city lights. I'd be all alone in the house, and look across at the trees on the far bank, and it was hard to think it was the same water. It was hard to think it was the same lights, from just up the bend, that seemed so close."

"That's right," Goat said, turning to her intimately, as though she were the only one who understood. He picked up a little carrot from the crudités on the table and held it out as though to feed it to her. With deft fingers she took it and held it in a closed fist.

I saw a looming managerial type put his head in the doorway. Ignored there, he stepped in. He looked like he might have been an old player, but I couldn't place him. "Fifteen minutes, folks," he said.

"Anybody want to go to the bathroom?" X Games asked, pulling out a showy lighter. "Last chance."

I went out beyond the glass to the real seats and stood watching the janitors work. The most famous building in the city had the look of an empty festival-ground, getting swept for popcorn and soda cups. The scoreboard still showed the Blazers' victory, but the digital ads beneath the scorer's table had been turned off. All the hokey signs of allegiance remained, presiding over the empty rows: there was a group of seats marked *Przybilla's Posse*, and the *Aldridge Army*, awaiting the return of the departed host. There was even one for Calyph, a small swath in the corner under the banner of *West's Warriors*. I wondered if I could sneak away a second, and call somebody anonymously from a pay phone and get them to go bring him inside, so he wouldn't go and catch the flu if it rained. It might be bad for his knee to be out there. There might be an exercise he couldn't do or some meds he was missing.

I heard the door slide open and Goat came and stood alongside me.

"We're going to the Gaucho. You know you're coming."

"I don't know," I said.

"Antonia says you have to. She won't come without you."

I turned on him. The fuzz of his new mustache gave him the look of a stretched-out undergraduate looking for a score. "Make this one memorable with somebody else," I said.

He put his hand on my shoulder and gave me his tired, inexhaustible smile. "It isn't like that," he assured me. "We've been through a lot together, right? You and me both. Just one drink, Jess."

In the lounges of El Gaucho it was happy hour all night. Half-drunk already on arena rail liquor, even Goat's parental stand-ins clamored for top-shelf. When I tried to get a coffee, Goat shouted me down and I was given a Spanish. Behind us a guitarist played placidly on, as though it would be his pleasure to ignore all behaviors at all volumes.

Goat kept bringing over spare chairs. "Some of the guys are coming," he'd say, as though we'd all fixed our hopes on this and he didn't want anyone to lose faith. "My new brothers!"

"No brothers in Toronto but Joe Carter."

"More than here! Shouldn't some of our guys be around?"

"They go to the cigar lounge," Antonia said. "It's private."

She rose to go to the bathroom, and Goat sent several chairs clattering backward as he stood to head her off.

"They don't let you go alone in here," he cried. She put her hand on his shoulder, to soothe him and fix him to his spot, and we watched her go across the room.

"They won't let her," Goat muttered.

Sure enough, as she was about to leave the bar a black-jacketed waiter materialized to accompany her.

"I'ma bring her back," he declared, but his X Games friend stood and said something in his ear. Obviously sulking, Goat turned to me.

"You got a girl's name, Jess. You try it."

Somebody made that long *oh* sound frat boys make when someone's picked a fight or brought a new insult into the world, and I figured I didn't want to abide the table anyhow.

"Okay," I said. I picked up Antonia's purse to further laughter, but when I slung it around my shoulder, Goat's eyes widened a little—he needed Antonia to remind him he was having a good time, and he wasn't going to miss a trick from anyone who might try to take her away.

"One at a time," he cried, but I was up and gone already.

I went through the dining room to the back, and as I stepped through a doorway I smelled cigar smoke. I saw a core of ash bobbing softly in a corner next to a red lamp, gleaming above a dull pair of shoes. Above it was the sleepy face of the Pharaoh. He lifted one eyebrow slightly and looked at me with hooded, impassive eyes. Then he started to laugh soundlessly.

"Nice purse," he said.

I took it off my shoulder and held it bunched in my hand. "This the men's line?"

"I think we need to have a talk, you and me."

"I'm in a hurry," I said. "Talk away."

The men's opened and Wedge stepped out.

"Not that kind of talk, ma'fucka," Pharaoh said softly. He came off the wall and loomed comfortably in front of me. I could feel Wedge behind me, and I said I guessed I could spare just a minute.

I've always thought of myself as someone with a great and tenacious will to live, the sort who if dropped into the ocean for five days would cheerfully hang on to the stinking, half-eaten carcass of a whale, and even gnaw it himself, to get back to the human world and all the things he'd left undone. But in the rare cases when someone's so much as suggested the assertion of their physical will, I never fight it at all—I just go along gracefully and tell myself it probably isn't serious. Pharaoh walked ahead of me, and Wedge behind, and we went into the lounge to a corner booth without a hand being laid on me. When I die

I'll probably go so quietly it'll be like I made it my last trick to struggle the least of anyone, to feign the utmost peace.

"What you doin' with Leef's girl?" Pharaoh was sipping from a copper cup and pulling on his cigar, and though he did both slowly, he moved from one to the other so regularly I didn't see where he got the breathing in.

"I work for her, too," I said.

I felt a waiter appear over my shoulder. "Chateaubriand and an ostrich filet," he recited in a proud, muted tone.

"You bring that '57?"

"Yessir. Anything for this gentleman?"

"He'll have a mineral water," Pharaoh rasped. "So?"

"She was at the game with your friend Goat. She wanted me to come get her out of here."

Pharaoh made an impatient noise. "You think Leef and her gon get back together?"

"Why do you care?"

He looked at me in ridicule and gave a short laugh. "For his happiness, ma'fucka. Why you think?"

I didn't think he knew what I knew, and I couldn't tell if he was sincere.

"I think they might," I said.

Pharaoh looked at Wedge with a hard twitch of his lips you couldn't call a smile. "Nah," he said. "I think you wrong there."

"Okay."

"You wanna make a bet?"

"No," I said.

"I'll lay you real good odds. How 'bout this. Wedge here will stake you two hundred at ten-to-one they don't. He ain't even want a cut. Then I'll show you how to make it happen. Easy money, right?"

"That's two grand," I said.

"Boy can count." Pharaoh laughed mirthlessly, uncapping his sauce.

I looked down at the mineral water that had appeared. I was sure it would taste like brine. "I thought your issue was his happiness."

"It is," he said. "I don't wanna see it no more." He put a cut of steak into his mouth and chewed in violent satisfaction.

"I hear you're going to marry Odette," I said. I just meant to delay him for a minute, to parse the Pharaoh's sudden change from a vague malevolence to a specific one. He seemed to know, all right.

He stared at me in disdain as he hurried to swallow. "I can't marry no white girl," he said finally, wiping his lips and throwing down the napkin.

"And Calyph shouldn't either?"

"It ain't good for us."

"Why?"

He put down his fork, and for a second he looked only discouraged. "You ain't about to understand," he rasped.

"I'll take your bet if you just tell me why."

He shook his head. "You got any wisdom on this piece, Dub? Why wouldn't you marry a white girl?"

Wedge paused with a slice of ostrich halfway to his mouth. "W. E. B. Du Bois say," he said, and then he put the meat in his mouth and chewed thoughtfully. He kept his eyes on me as he ate, and then he swallowed and wiped his mouth politely on the white cloth napkin. "He say never marry a girl who let you ass-fuck." Then he winked.

Pharaoh nodded solemnly and leaned forward into the candlelight. "You need us to ship you any more of our voodoo know-how, you just ask. In the meantime, can we get on?"

I felt a strange humiliation, like I was just the latest in a line of white people who came awkwardly into their world, trying to appear natural, looking for the ultimate truths they had failed to find in their own neighborhoods.

"But what did he ever do to you?" I asked.

"Same thing you tried a couple weeks back."

"She probably just went to him," I said softly, "since you don't want her."

The Pharaoh glared at me furiously. "Listen, mother—"

"I want five," I said.

Wedge gave a high laugh and put out his hand as if to give me a slap upside.

"Leave the fool be," Pharaoh said, instantly all hard business again. "I'd need pictures for five."

"How do you want it done?" I asked. I don't think I had any real idea yet what he wanted of me.

"However you want. I just want pictures, and I want 'em to show shit, and I want 'em to be good. Get yo megapixels all over that. I don't want there to be any question."

"All right," I said vaguely. "I'll look into it. If she's into it, okay."

"Into it!" Pharaoh laughed. "Ma'fucka, you think we gon be relyin' on yo charm here?"

Wedge reached into his coat and slid an envelope across the table. Inside was a yellow slip of paper, a key, and a small vial.

"This here is a little Georgia Home Boy. The other is if you need a quiet place to go. Use it or not. Address is in there, and a number to call when you done it. You don't know what to do with Georgia, I don't know what to tell you."

I felt the hairs rising of the backs of my hands. "I know," I said.

Wedge gave me a backhand wave and I stood up. At the door I stopped and looked back through the mellow smoke. As I watched, the Pharaoh ground out his cigar and pushed his plate slowly away, as if these appetites had all been for show, and lifted his dull cup to drink.

When I got back to the public lounge, the food was just arriving, and Goat opened his arms as though to magnify the generosity of the spread. "Where you been?"

"Long line for the ladies."

Antonia looked at me curiously as she took back her purse.

Goat threw his arm abruptly around me. "I'm going to give this guy a job soon, if he can learn kilometers."

"I got a job," I muttered.

Antonia waited for Goat's attention to turn. "What's that about?" she asked in a low voice. Returned to her familiar presence, those things the Pharaoh wanted seemed to belong to a lurid world beyond reason. No one would want to do that to Antonia.

"I gave my notice a little while ago. It's nothing."

"You what? Why?"

I explained about Pharaoh and Joseph Jones, how our week there had come with a pitch and they wanted everyone to have Lost Boys. "I didn't want to get in the way," I said.

"Don't you need the money?"

"I'll be all right."

"Let me guess. Your fallen family left you a trust?"

"Yeah. Well, sort of. It's—"

"I don't know how you get Calyph to believe any of that shit," she said abruptly. "Anyway, you had it pretty good with us. I don't see why you'd want to work for Lucas."

I stared at her, and she looked back at me coolly. I couldn't decide whether to protest or just to give it up. Of course she'd known all along that I had no such family, that I was making it up—her whole past was an instruction on the fine gradations between the few people who were like her and all the rest who were not.

"They thought I fooled around with the Pharaoh's girl," I said at last. "Now don't feel sorry for me."

She seemed to stare yet harder, and where I hoped I'd see confusion, or even a little wounded pride that my touch of home-wrecking was not exclusive to her, there was only an intent disbelief, almost joyful in its dubiousness. "You don't expect me to believe that, either, do you? You don't even like girls."

I felt my eyelids peeling back. A wave of numb lulled through my legs. I shook my head, I tried to talk, but there were only a hundred little fragments of unfit things to say.

"You know who you really want," she added.

Again I stuttered. I felt my tongue moving behind my teeth, trying to get some traction. But I could only stare. I felt my face pull close to hers.

"Oh, admit it," she said, narrowing her eyes joyfully.

"Can't I want everything?" I managed finally.

She looked at me doubtfully, not as if she disbelieved me but as if she saw right away how little value there was in everything. She must have known all too well that to want it all was a desire fit only for summer songs. I'd wanted nothing in particular for so long, and then I'd found them, and a focus at last. They'd given me the whole world new again, and now it was theirs that was lifeless and declining.

"I'll prove what I want," I said. "I'll prove what I am."

"All right," she said, giving half a laugh. "Anything to get out of here."

I drank the rest of my Spanish and stood. Goat sensed something and looked over with a piece of cheese in his teeth.

"We out," I told him.

"What?"

I threw what money I had down on the table. "Thanks for the box. I'll be in touch."

"Where you going?"

"I'm taking this one home," I said.

"Let's all go," Goat said quickly. "Let's all go someplace else."

"We got to get home," I repeated, hearing that rhythm creep into my voice. It was Calyph's of course, but it was so suited for the moment, stripped down and empowered. I felt undeniable.

"It was good to see you again, Lucas," she said.

She took my arm and we went past the solemn musician toward the door.

She glanced back. "Oh God, he's getting up."

"Where's his car?"

"I'm sure he won't follow us," she said doubtfully.

Out on the pavement she jogged ahead of me. "This," I said, pointing to my sad ride. "See what they left me with?"

She got her own door and slid in the front. "You shouldn't have let that lisping girl do those things to you," she said, drawing the belt quickly over her.

"She's degraded," I told her. "You can't believe anything she says."

I started the car and we came back south along Broadway. As we went by the Gaucho, I saw Goat on the sidewalk. Antonia made a pained face and put her hand up to shield herself.

"There's no way he's actually coming after us."

At Taylor we had to stop for a light. The yellow came on me suddenly, and Antonia pitched forward a little and looked over, appraising.

"I'm fine," I said. "Spanishes perk you up."

We were alone at the line and the car felt exposed in the middle of the street. A pigeon pecked a drunken circle at the crosswalk's edge. When the light turned again, I thought I heard a roar coming on us from behind.

I could've turned down the next street—I could've gone down Salmon to Naito to Macadam home. It could've all been avoided. But I knew how to drive. I wasn't afraid.

As we went by the concert hall, I saw the Maybach behind us. I took my foot off a little and it roared up, with the ghostly float of a broad car with an overlarge engine. One of its headlights had burned out, and the remaining shone out dazzlingly, like he'd gone to the brights to compensate.

She made a scoffing sound. "That's someone else."

"Weren't you just in his car?"

He began to honk.

She gave a little sigh. "I guess we could pull over and see."

"Naw," I said. "I got this."

Down toward Market I started to slow, watching the cross-walk lights, looking for a yellow to jump. The walks were blinking deeper into their count each block. They were all timed—if you went steady you could sail right through downtown, and I picked up speed as slowly as I could as the Maybach floated nearer.

Under the PSU overpass a yellow came while we were still half a block short. "You're safe with me," I said, and then I hit it. It clicked red just as I went through, but Goat blew through behind me in a blast of scorched soy.

A freeway ramp lay ahead, and I got into the exit lane like I was going to take it and then juked back at the last minute. The Maybach had fallen back a little, and stayed smoothly behind. Next was the five-corners leading onto 99, and again I juked coming up to the light and shot off, out of the main stream, toward Broadway Drive and the southwest hills. It was my last real chance to lose him all at once, and this time his tires screamed out in blatant pursuit.

"I guess it's possible that's him," Antonia allowed. She'd pulled a piece of gum from somewhere and was chewing it wildly.

The narrow road wound sharply and we were losing speed, struggling up between the dark terraced houses and sudden trees. The Mazda's engine was no fit for an uphill chase, but I didn't know if the Maybach could handle it or if the bio-fit slowed it at all—and I knew the roads. Above us was Council Crest, the highest lookout point in the city, and as we sped toward it through a warren of twisted old streets, I built up a lead until all I could see of the other car was the side of its single, overbright beam, pointing at things other than us.

There was a fork at the entrance to the park, with one road leading down again to the city. I counted on losing him there— the park itself was a dead end, and I veered off, into the streets that twisted down and away. I could feel her beside me, hanging on, one hand on the door and the other on the side of my seat. His headlight faded, my rearview was dark, and all at once I felt the fun of it all. Just that day I'd held a spear; I'd broken into her house and she had no idea. I'd won at a car chase and seen ostrich eaten and imposed myself a little at last on the vast soft surface of the indifferent earth. For so many years I'd assumed the ground beneath me so impenetrable it wasn't even worth challenging, but suddenly I saw that it was soft, so soft in the hands of any willful man. I could become new and new and new.

"Could you not . . ." Antonia said. I must have been unconsciously revving or something. I could hear the gum held tightly between her teeth.

"What?" I asked. I turned and looked at her and held the look as I made my efficient and professional way down toward the city, with all its strong and its broken homes, their lights blending together below us indistinguishably.

"Nothing," she said. "Good work. Take me home."

"Oh yes ma'am," I said.

We reached a length of straight decline and I let us coast, cracking the window to take the air. I felt the wet earth beneath the trees, and my fast blood. I thought of which house of the three I'd most like to go to, and sighed at the banquet before me, and reached down to click the child locks in place.

The locks had moved, though. I must've been feeling so Jag I forgot which car I was in. I had to reach down and feel around a little. It was no trouble, not at first, when it was just another winking light at the bottom of the hill, blended with the house-lights. Even as it grew, I didn't think much of it. To be in front of us now, Goat would have to either be a savant or so addled it wasn't worth pondering. By the time I got the locks, the light had come up pretty near—it looked like a motorcycle out for a late ride. Then I watched the light twist at the strangest angle, like the lamp was separating from its housing, and it swept over me and I turned to see the light pass over Antonia's terrified face. I could see the fine colorless hairs above her lip, and within her nose, and then with impossible suddenness the broad sidewall of the Maybach swept in front of us, and the air broke loose with angry metal birds. I felt my arm fly out, a thin thing I every day passed up the chance to strengthen, and my hand closed over hers on the far door's handle, but I knew it wouldn't hold.

10

Before the hospital, there was just a little pain, and a new looseness in my arm I didn't want to think too hard about. Before the reckoning, there was just her still-warm seat and her chewing gum flat against the windshield, and before the search that came before all that, there was just the feeling that it wasn't such a bad crash and that she'd somehow ended up lying gracefully on top of me in a long white dress. The car was very quiet and I didn't want to open my eyes. We seemed to be at peace in stillness and in movement at once, like we'd run a long way to a pier at the edge of the world and thrown ourselves onto the deck of a great ship just as it was leaving, and now could rest as it carried us out amid the white noise of its massive peace, through the island wilderness, a continent unto itself, bearing us across the sea. And then I reached out with my good arm to touch her gently wherever my pure, protecting hand should fall, and of course it was just the air bag that had made her seem so light and near.

I opened my eyes, and my dread was made visible and crept along the edges of my vision like some millipede mounting a bank of black muck. I made myself turn and look at her, and she wasn't there at all.

This seemed, at first, a slight relief. I could have opened my eyes on anything, anything: some foreign matter like uncooked sausage spread over the dashboard, fragments of teeth sunk into the cheap plastic of the glove box, her soft hair covering a head no longer quite round. And though I could do nothing to shield her from any man manic enough to come head-on into our lane in his massively heavy car, to have seen so much as a broken finger or a thin stream of blood dripping quietly from her nose would have been unendurable. Because even if I was just some deviant aspirant to the servant class, worming into the heart of their days with my amateur manners, they had put their lives in my hands, from the first day, and hers was, with our lingering patriarchy and her little bones, the more delicate life, and I had not even tried to stop. He'd come on us and my only feeling was a sort of indignation, a desire to backhand his faulty life choices out of our way and keep on, suave and undeterred. I wasn't willing to credit his hulking car even with being cause for alarm, and had tried to dodge him casually along the shoulder. We'd gone head-on and I hadn't once touched the brake.

But then I looked again, and her absence was no relief anymore.

The air bag, deflated now, hung over her seat like an insufficient parachute. I registered optimistically that it wasn't discolored with any kind of fluid, and the windshield too was pure, save for a single crack, long and clean, and then her chewing gum, fixed against the glass. I touched it with the tip of my finger and it felt cemented on. At what speed must it have left her, to land there before the bag could deploy?

I looked out through the split windshield for some sign of Goat's car in the skewed glare of our surviving headlight, but the road was all dark. She'd been belted in. I sat a minute, uncomprehending. Then I saw a bit of colored paper stuck beneath the wipers.

I got out, tilting my head so I'd not have to look at my arm. When I opened the door, some shards fell from the stump of rearview and joined the litter of plastic and glass on the roadway. Our narrow bumper lay mangled in the damp earth a little ways off, seeming to shrug in apology. Next to it a trail of long foot-prints ran through the soft earth along her side of the car.

I pulled the paper from the windshield, which gave a little when I pressed on it. Written in shaky caps over the print on the back of a taco coupon were the words "GONE 4 HELP."

On any other day, in any other circumstance of my ordinary life, I might've been able to sit and wait. The small wisdom I'd gleaned from my history of accidents suggested the passive ap-proach was a sound one, and I expect I could in any other season have quietly patted myself down for undiscovered internal inju-ries, reached for my phone to make sure someone was coming, and then leaned back in my seat in the hopped-up relaxation of a superficially mangled man who has escaped death, and dreamed consolatory daydreams of all the ways it could have been worse.

I took the sleeve of my good arm between my teeth and grit-ted down on it, in a weakling's preparation for a difficult busi-ness, and then I pulled up my other sleeve and looked at my elbow. There was an ugly well of color on the inside of the joint, but no bones seemed out of place and nothing had broken the skin. I've never had any tolerance for pain, and I knew I'd need a hospital in time, but none of that felt pressing when my arm smelled faintly of her perfume.

I tried to start the car, expecting silence, or at most a grinding denial of a sound that kept on as long as I could turn the key, but after a moment the engine woke smoothly, miraculously to life. I turned back to the road and the wheels shrieked against the bent frame. About a third of the front end was crumpled in, the remaining headlight gave almost no help, and I was leaking air and who knew what else, but so long as I never saw a cop or had to make a turn I thought I might make it part of the way to wherever I was going.

A few blocks back toward the city, I saw the gleam of newly

spilled gas and figured Goat had gone the same way. I flipped on the brights and the fog lights to try to follow his leaks, and got almost to the fork between the OHSU hospital and downtown before I saw another car. It honked at me in three short bursts, and I slowed and shut off the brights until it passed. When I turned them on once more, it was just in time to see a few drops of yellowish fluid lead me away from the turnoff to the hospital.

When choosing between incompetence and malice to explain the mistakes of others, a life in the softer parts of the most comfortable America has mostly led me to the former. I've always had it in the back of my mind that further experience would reveal people to be much more twisted than I'd so far seen, but I'd walked many years among the middle of the middle keeping up the self-satisfied feeling that a basic empathy could be found for nearly anyone, while I waited for my naïveté to be punctured. Still, that day I was hurt like I'd rarely been hurt, and guilty like never before. It was possible Goat just didn't know where the nearest emergency room was, but as I crept back toward the center of the city, feeling the throb build in my arm, it seemed more and more like he wasn't taking her to a hospital at all.

In the industrial south end I pulled over as gradually as possible and took the GHB from my pocket. It was a cap full of clear liquid, as innocuous as anything in a vial can be. I picked up the key and turned it in my hand. It was chainless, so bright and new that I could imagine it hanging uncut that very day in a hardware store. I wondered how many others like it had been made.

Sure my call would go unanswered, I picked up my phone and tried her. After the third ring, there was a click and I thought I heard breathing. Then the phone slid away, and there was only dirty noise, a passing bass beat, and the unintelligible exuberance of some far-off kid telling the universe his plans. I looked at the address on the yellow slip and put the car in gear again.

It was a street off Killingsworth, in one of the old black neighborhoods. Renewal was a ways off there yet, a promise but not yet a fear, and the main blocks felt thick with the life of all the folks pushed there by our initiatives elsewhere. Goat's mangled car was parked in the driveway of the house, the destruction evident even from behind. I went on by and the street kids who'd been gathered around the horror of his ride exclaimed in delight at the horror of mine. I went around the corner, the dread thickening again in my throat.

I popped the trunk, hoping there'd be a lug wrench or something to wield, but in the well with the spare there was just a can of Fix-a-Flat. I found one of Calyph's team hoodies in a pile of old clothes and slipped it gingerly on.

When I came around the block, the kids were coming toward me, talking about the Maybach, what a nice ride it was and what a shame someone had gone and done that to it. "We could tear the rims off and boy wouldn't even *notice*," the tallest one said. I walked right by them on the grass and they didn't look at me; with the hood up I was transformed into a routine neighborhood figure.

One yard over from the house I stopped under the block's only tree. There was a light burning in a window off the porch but no sign of movement. Pharaoh's car was nowhere to be seen, but if Goat was doing what I feared I couldn't imagine he had help.

The door was unlocked and the front room empty, but in the bedroom off the porch I found her facedown and unmoving with her torn underwear round her ankles. Her wrists were curled together under her chin, as if she had fallen asleep somewhere safer. Her dress was pulled up to her ribs. The room was bare but for a double mattress laid on the floor, an industrial work lamp that covered the room with harsh, barred light, and a blinking radio crudely simulating the sound of a train.

I knelt on the mattress. When I touched her cheek her face remained slack and senseless, and I put the back of my hand beneath her nose as I'd seen done in some film. She was breathing. After I shook her she just lay where she fell.

She wasn't bound and I couldn't see any sign of struggle but for the tear in her silks. Both her knees and the heel of one of her hands looked swollen, from the crash I supposed, along with the belt bruise that purpled already across her waist. I knew what I must check next, but I wasn't sure if I should turn her or what. Hearing my breath loud in my nose I leaned back and turned her hips and looked. She looked undisturbed, the soft hair unmatted, through it was hard to be sure.

I stood again and glanced out, but the front room was quiet. Looking round the room, I snatched up a short length of wooden curtain rod from above the window.

It was a tiny bungalow of a house and there weren't many places for him to be. A drained fish tank in the main room let out a dull blue glow, and the only other light in the place came from beneath the bathroom door. I stopped a moment outside the back bedroom, in case he was making preparations in the black, but then I heard the toilet flush.

When I was small I once picked the lock of the bathroom door with a butter knife, and I remember my mother explaining that these doors couldn't be serious because otherwise children with greater initiative than I might hole up behind them and drink all the poisons under the sink. I put my foot to the door and it flew inward; I heard the inner knob puncture the wall plaster. I had the jump on him perfectly, but it was impossible. He was sitting on the toilet, pants down, with a long-lensed camera around his neck and blood running down his face, crying. When he saw me he put his hand up to his crotch to hide himself within the porcelain, and I felt with wild certainty that he'd just finished jerking himself off into the bowl. He turned his face away in shame, like a beaten paparazzo, and I saw his nose was misshapen and likely broken.

"I only wanted the pictures," he whimpered.

"How bad is she hurt?"

"She hit me," he cried piteously, holding his free hand up to the blood slowly sheeting from his nose. "Look at this. I was never going to do anything."

"He gave you a vial, too," I said.

He nodded, sniffing, then abruptly reached around for something to cover himself. There were no towels, and he stretched down and took up the stained bathmat and set it in place. Its fringe drooped over his lap pathetically.

"How was she when you took her?"

"Fine. She's fine. She was out and then she woke and I told her we were going to the hospital. She said she felt sleepy but I thought it was just the stuff."

I had a brief image of him feeding knockout drugs to an unconscious person I vaguely loved. "Give me that camera," I said.

He reached for the strap obediently. "There's nothing on it." But as he lifted it over his head I saw him hit a button with his thumb.

"Good," I said. Then I turned it on again and took a picture of him. I took up the rod and smashed it into the sink to get his attention, sending the plastic round the cold tap into pieces. He cowered and I took another.

"For a few thousand," I said. "If he went ten you'd have made a snuff film?"

"You think I'm doing this for a check?" he said, almost haughtily. "I owed him, after that servant girl. He knows enough people, I'd be done if I didn't square with him."

"You make great amends," I said.

At the first whiff of moral judgment he lapsed again into self-pity. "Oh God, I'm not like this. You know I'd never touch her. You know me. I'm a feminist."

With this appeal he rose off his seat a little and stretched his arms out, compelling my belief. When he settled again, something in his pants clinked.

"That's just my keys," he said quickly.

I tapped the curtain rod against my knee, and with a sigh he let a pair of handcuffs leak out onto the floor.

"He gave them to me," he mumbled.

"Good," I said. "Hook yourself to that sink and then you can clean yourself up."

"Here? I got to get to the hospital. You think I want to wear a face mask all season?"

I lifted the camera. "Link up and you get this back. We'll call you an ambulance."

He frowned and bunched the cuffs in his fist like he was thinking of bucking me. I couldn't tell if he knew about my arm, but even if I was healthy, he was still an athlete facing a man with a curtain rod. My only real instrument of control was his shame, his ever-fleeting shame. Any moment he could forgive himself and forget his humiliation, and after that I knew my chances weren't good.

I tugged the hood forward as far as it would go and laid the rod against the sink. "Come on," I said, in my best hard voice. "She needs a hospital."

Reluctantly he linked one cuff to himself, but I didn't hear a click. Then without warning he stood up slowly, tossing off the mat and hitching his pants as the cuffs fell to the floor.

"Say, why didn't you stop your car up there?" he said, his voice suddenly dangerous with the delusion of reason. "You're some driver. We could've all been killed!"

"Why didn't *I*?"

"I left you plenty of room to stop," he assured me, and then he reached out and gave me a hard, brotherly clap on the arm and I heard myself cry out in pain.

"Whoa there, son," he said. "You hurt, too?"

"Hey," I heard a voice whisper behind me. "Hey, guys."

She was standing in the hall at the edge of the light, her face partly in shadow, so you could only see her mouth and the hollow of her throat, and then her crumpled dress, in place now, and beneath her puffy, discolored knees.

"Hey, girl," Goat said. "You feeling better?"

Something in the set of her mouth made me stand aside.

"What happened to your face?" she asked him.

"I got into a car accident," he said. "Now we're all going to the hospital."

I was between them and trying to look at both of them and then I felt her hand on mine, and a tug at the rod.

"Hey," she said to Goat. "Say that again. Say 'Hey, girl.'"

"What?" He smiled like she was making a joke he didn't understand.

Again there was a tug at the rod, and I loosed my grip.

"Say 'Hey,'" she said.

Her face came into the light, the rod upraised in her hand. He put his hands up, ready to stop the blow, but she held the rod too high, and the tip glanced against the door frame and rebounded back. She felt it and crouched as she rushed at him, and hit him low with the knob held in her fist. His face popped with agony and surprise, but she'd gone to her knees, and he reached down and his hand came up full of her hair. I watched the look come across his broken face, with its small mustache stained with clotted blood, the wild look of a man gone beyond his knowledge of himself into some new, instinctual place, and as he pulled her head back so her face was upraised he brought his other hand up fisted and backhanded, and I was moving. As I reached out to block the stroke, I knew myself again as I always had, a clumsy man of inaction, but I knew, too, that I was the one making the amends, while he was just cornered with the knowledge of his accumulated idiocy and wrongdoing, forced to play out a role even he must have been surprised to find was part of his destiny, and maybe the slower for that, and so maybe I would get there in time.

His sweeping fist caught on my forearm, and I put my elbow on his nose with what seemed an inadequate motion. I must have disturbed some of the looser bones of his face, because he cried out again and swayed on his heels. With Antonia blocking his knees, I pulled him forward and he toppled over her to the ground.

As I saw him go down I wondered if he'd just give up, go fetal with a groaning concession, because he had once been a decent guy who must feel pained to be so deeply in the wrong, and taking so much abuse for it. Instead he tried to bite some of my fingers off. Antonia got the stick on him like she'd taken a class for it and I sort of laid on his shoulders, managing an eventual homeschool half nelson and yelling for her to cuff his leg. He thrashed against that idea awhile until finally she gave him a pop on the kneecap and said stop it and he did and we cuffed him to the sinkpipe. Then she crawled out of his range into the dark of the hall, and went promptly to sleep again. Bracing my distended elbow against my side, I lifted her and put her over my shoulder, and we went out into the night and the grimy street, and when halfway down the walk her weight shifted and I thought I would drop her, the gang of kids who had come back again to gape at Goat's shattered car ran over and held her, and helped me bear her on.

"I'd like a cup of tea before bed, I think."

She leaned back against the cracked headrest, pressing an ice pack to her wrist. Two more hung strapped with blue bands to her knees, the deflated air bag brushing against her legs with the rhythm of the road. Antonia was a towel and a stool away from a postgame interview, but the hospital had said to come back in the morning, it probably wasn't anything more than a mild concussion, and I had saved her, or something like that, or she me. Saving had happened and I'd been there. The worst had been possible and now it wasn't anymore. Now the world was returned again to its customary plenitude of quiet and insidious wrongs ripe to be temporarily overlooked.

"Of course," I said. "I'll make you some tea."

"Or maybe some hot milk. My throat burns."

"I'll get you some nice hot milk," I said almost automatically, and she looked over at me with faint irony.

"I still don't understand why you made that up about your family."

I'd confessed in the waiting room, before the ice and the pills, and the tests for her and the sling for me, to keep her awake, because it seemed time, and because she knew anyway. I even made her promise not to tell Calyph, more to save him the embarrassment of having believed me than anything.

"How'd you really grow up?" she asked.

I shrugged. "My father installed water heaters. He and my mom died snowmobiling when I was six. I didn't want to bore you with that."

"You should have. We'd have hired you anyhow," she said reproachfully. "You saved our cat."

Beneath us the car rattled dangerously. I knew it wasn't streetworthy, and soon they would say it was totaled, but I needed a few more miles. I knew it was the last time I'd drive for either of them.

"Where are we going?" she asked.

"Home," I said.

She looked at me skeptically, as if to say, I hurt and am cold, don't fuck with me here.

"It's all right," I said. "He's gone. The place is empty."

"I don't live there anymore, Jess."

"You've still got a key, right?"

When we came to the security gates, they were closed, and I tried to remember if I'd done it myself or if that meant he really was gone, searching for me somewhere between the green spaces and the grid with an SUV full of dangerous men. We pulled up the drive and I knew I'd have no answer if the house was blazing with lights, if the police were there. Going around a bend I saw a glow, but it was just a faint spill across the Linux man's lawn—the house was dark and the garage closed. The car knocked terminally to a halt and we sat a moment in the quiet.

"You think he's still chained to the sink?"

I shrugged. I'd called 911 from the hospital and the operator had been confused. "He'll look good in a face mask," I said. "Guys wear it for style now."

"I really don't remember doing that to his face."

"The world leagues will thank you," I said, and it was true—by January he would be signed by CSKA Moscow.

I undid the child locks and our doors squeaked open. She stood in the drive a moment, looking up at the dark house with the key in her hand.

"Are you sure?"

"Sure I'm sure," I said.

She walked gingerly up the front steps, the ice melt sloshing around her knees. I told her I'd only be a minute and went around to the back door of the garage. The Jaguar was still there. I put my hand on the hood and it was cold. The tires didn't look newly chalked.

I stepped quickly into the house, where a light bloomed up-stairs.

"Hello?" My voice came out hoarsely.

"In the bedroom," she called.

"Come down and have tea."

"In a minute."

I found a kettle and put on some water, and then I went and glanced in a few rooms, looking for any sign of him. Everything was peaceful save for my own disorder—the dried spittle on the photograph looked like Angel Falls. I picked up the poker I'd flung on the floor and put it back in its rack. If only the balcony floor were wooden, I could've gone outside and put a light through the slats and known.

She came down the stairs just as the kettle began to whistle. She'd changed into a mismatched sleep outfit. Her shirt had the name of some electronics store, with a plug coming out of an "s" and wrapping around to underline the name. Her pajama bottoms had shamrocks. The ice packs around her knees had been replaced by two bags of frozen peas.

"I miss that cat," she announced and went to the fridge for milk.

I tried to go for the tea, but I didn't know where anything was and she shooed me off. "I'm indestructible," she said. "Sit down. What kind do you want?"

"Earl Grey," I said, and she smiled a little at the stage quality of the response. When it was ready she gave me the little tray, which I could just manage with one hand, and with the tiny pitcher of cream rattling against the sugar bowl we went up the stairs.

She'd straightened the room so there wasn't any trace of the morning. The bed was made again and the closet door closed. It looked like the master bedroom of any big suburban home, waiting to soften any of ten thousand soft lives.

"Can you believe there was a spear in here? The one from the armor. It was just lying on the floor."

I put on a broad, quizzical look. Already I was moving over to the curtains, which were just half closed. I couldn't find the line to draw them fully shut, and my hand fumbled uselessly within the fabric.

"What'd you do with it?" I asked, feeling up and down.

"I just rolled it under the bed. There was a first-aid kit under there, too. The bachelor life."

At last I found the cord. Before drawing the curtains I looked out, but the spill of light was empty and beyond there was nothing visible.

I took up my cup and sipped, gazing down at the stained undershirt I'd stripped down to when they'd put the sling on.

"Have you got a robe or something?"

"Sure." She went to the closet and drew out a deep-red robe, cut so long of such thick terrycloth that it was halfway to being some animal pelt, fringed with a vestige of the beast.

Handing it to me, she climbed onto the bed, propping the pillows behind her. I thought with familiar longing how easy it would be to put on the robe, to lie next to her and show her the spot on my thigh where her cat had bitten me, boast of breaking into her house, and tell her how tenderly I'd examined her delicate, insensate body. She was very tired, and probably wouldn't take any of it seriously, but who knew how long and how far I could play the role of the usurping husband before the outside world caught up with us? But I knew I had no place with her. She had to learn how to be rich in the America of now, without delusion or embarrassment, and needed to be with those who could show her how. I had to go off and buy a plant or something, and learn how not to kill it or creep it out, and find a new small room to live in, where I could settle at last into my blanched and soon youthless skin, the skin of the past refusing to pass, the skin of obsolete conquerors and indifferent kings.

I slung the robe over my shoulder and went again to the glass, and as Antonia looked at me strangely I unlatched the door and drew it back.

"Who's there," he said instantly, in a weak, hoarse voice, and at the sound of his voice she gave a short cry.

We heard him scrape to his feet, and again Antonia cried out.

"It's all right," I said. My voice was casual. I felt nonchalant, with a strange, light feeling of relief.

"I guess he's home after all," I said. I felt the heft of the robe in my hand, and thought how heavy it would have been around my shoulders. Without it my body was deft and responsive, and I stepped back from the doorway and stood aside to let him through.

Calyph came in rubbing sleep from his eyes. His jacket was smirched and damp with dew, and he looked like a boy whose prom night had gone horribly wrong. I could see him straining to show that nothing bothered him, to have us know that every misfortune weak enough to happen in Dunthorpe was to be soaked up in stride. We exchanged a quick, uneasy glance. I could see his legs shaking through the tight slacks.

"Fell asleep," he announced.

Antonia lay on the bed, the mug of tea forgotten in her hand.

"Let's get you out of that coat," I said. I put my hand on his damp shoulder with easy familiarity, and he turned away from his wife and let me take it from him. When I brushed his hand it was as cold as if he'd soaked it in ice water. The tips of his fingers looked swollen and bruised, and I wondered if he'd tried to pry his way back inside.

I laid down the coat and took up the robe and spread it as wide as my arm allowed. He squared himself and looked at me over his shoulder, watchful and hard. He looked at my bad arm and he seemed to be contemplating something, something surely terrible, and softly I laid the robe over his shoulders, to forestall him.

"I'll let you change," I said, as he put his arms through, and giving a small nod to Antonia, who was still staring at us from over the steaming cup, the packs of peas bunched carefully upon her knees, I went out of the room and shut the door behind me, and went down the stairs toward the garage, and the little room they'd given me for my own.

11

I didn't know they were really back together until late the next morning, when I strolled into the mudroom and nearly went nose-over on the sleeping body of the serval. It horked to life and tore through the hall, and then it was being yelled at for damaging the Ninth Ward photo, and defended with meows that were all too human.

All the little sounds within the house seemed more familiar than ever that morning—even the quality of light felt more cheerful. The rows of coats and little shoes seemed to greet me, to accept me as a regular part of life there, and to promise that the people within felt the same. I suppose I even thought they might ask me to stay on.

But something went out of their faces when they saw me that day. They were standing in the kitchen, fully dressed, and when I came in they glanced at one another, as if in some confirmation, and when they looked back they both seemed farther away.

"Morning, J."

I yawned politely and adjusted the sling I'd worn to sleep. My elbow was badly swollen and it throbbed some, but the sling felt precautionary, and mostly a symbol of sacrifice.

Antonia proffered a large bottle of painkillers, and I took a few. "How's your head?" I asked.

"Meh," she reported.

Calyph cleared his throat. "Get something to eat," he said.

When I came back with a glass of juice, Antonia was looking

at her phone, and when I set the glass on the counter near her, she jumped back a little.

"How you sleep?" Calyph asked.

I settled onto my stool and laughed. "Have you ever actually been over there?"

"Sure," he said. "Sure."

"It's like a prison cell," I said.

Again Antonia shrank back from me slightly.

"Ras and them people did it up. We'd have done it better, if it was us."

"I guess it's too late now," I said, willing them to say otherwise.

Calyph cleared his throat again. "Is your stuff packed up? We'll get you a ride back to your place when you're ready."

"I can drive myself."

"Ain't nobody in that kind of shape right now. We'll get you a ride out."

"It's no hurry," I said, sipping.

Antonia sighed a strange, drastic sigh.

Suddenly I was on my feet. I could feel what she meant quite clearly. I felt like crossing my arms but I couldn't, and willed myself to summon any kind of dignity. "If you want me gone, I'll go."

"It ain't that," Calyph said.

She was looking down at my glass blankly. "It *is* that," she said. It was very silent then. I could hear the distant metal whine of a far-off contractor sawing something in half.

"But I saved you," I said quietly.

Still she wouldn't look at me, and spoke slowly. "We just need some space right now. You've become very . . . involved . . . in our lives. We've talked it over, and we don't think we can have you quite as near anymore."

I looked over at Calyph wildly. "You already fired me once."

He wouldn't look at me, staring downward with his jaw clenched so the muscle stood out. For once in his life, he was silent.

"Why now?" I asked, hearing my voice break. "If it weren't for me—"

She lifted her eyes then, and looked at me very steadily. "We appreciate everything you've done for us," she said.

I could feel my hand go up to my neck with a jerk, my fingers worrying my spine.

"I know it ain't the best time to hear this, J. And we grateful for last night. I'm grateful. We just got to say goodbye now. We'll mail you a check."

"I don't understand."

Antonia opened her mouth, and her face was full of terrible clarity, as though just that morning she had realized something that had made her see the whole of our relations anew, and I was afraid, so afraid of what she would say, even though at the same time I had no idea what it would be, and felt, too, that there were no charges that could justly be laid before me—that I was their friend and had always meant the best. I was prepared at once to be revealed by some awful truth and to be indignant at it, at her utter misunderstanding of my intentions.

But she could say nothing. Her mouth shut again, and then they just looked at one another, helplessly, and from the drive came the sound of a door slamming.

"That's him," Antonia said.

"Who?"

"He'll take you home," Calyph said. "He'll take you wherever you want."

"But I still have nineteen days," I said hoarsely.

"Goodbye, Jess," they each said. "Goodbye." But they came no nearer, and softly beneath their words, I could hear what I had always known they would say one day: *Get out, get out.* And so I went, and in the driveway I met the man Mbakwe Trainor, called Nick, my replacement, who took me wordlessly and with great dignity back to my lesser home.

It was the end of November when my grandmother died and in Wisconsin the water in the ditches was turning to ice. The woman at the rental agency said that only two weeks past it'd been nearly seventy degrees and a warm fall wind the likes of which she'd never felt blew along the shores of Lake Michigan. But now the leaves that had even then been pinwheeled through McKinley Park by the gusts of summer undeparted shivered among the dry roadside grasses as Calyph and I drove southwest from General Mitchell into the reaped fields at the heart of the state.

I used to like a frozen November day. After I stopped playing football I stopped caring about the feeling of falling onto frozen ground, and watched the landscape stiffen with the satisfaction of someone safe in a warm place who is glad to see things moving along. Looking out the window, I tried to feel again that connection to the midwestern seasons flowing one into another. I used to get a sort of solace from the thought of the mice creeping beneath the threshing and the thawing sounds of unseen streams, but now the ground looked only harsh and colorless, just the dirt people made their numb way over, huddled in old blankets, eating cheese sausage, and running rusted space heaters behind the counters of little auto shops. Somehow I felt no loss in this differing vision—I had the feeling of seeing the natural beauty and natural ugliness together, and feeling equal pride in each.

"What's a salt lick?" Calyph asked, pressing ineffectually at the buttons of the rental's tiny, tacked-on navigation. He'd insisted on driving that day. He claimed his knee had got well enough to make it good exercise, and after the face he'd made at seeing the wrecked Mazda, I thought it best to go into retirement gracefully.

"Where'd you see that?"

"Just back there. Somebody wantin' to sell 'em off a plywood sign."

I looked backward pointlessly.

"Salt licks," he repeated. "Five dollars."

It took me a second to get over my surprise at his not knowing every damn thing in the world. "Salt lick's a block of salt for a deer," I told him.

"Huh! Is the salt as good? Or is it like some animal crude?"

"I never licked any," I said, feeling almost depressed at the impossibility of any other reply.

"You shoulda known people was gonna have these questions," he chided.

There was a pause in which I was supposed to have apologized, and then he went on. "Then they shoot the deer?"

"What?"

"Deer come for the salt and then they lamp it and shoot it."

"Is that what they do," I said.

"Isn't it?"

"That wouldn't be sporting," I said, adopting a patient, lecturing tone. "We have a code here. Not like the South."

"Oh, you got a code!" He laughed widely, all his teeth showing. It made him look crazed and dangerous, but it was his purest laugh.

I nodded solemnly.

"Who I know gonna teach me that? Andrew Bogut?"

I ignored this taunt. "I'm gonna teach you. And you'll have to learn, if you want anybody to respect you in this world."

Again he laughed crazily. "You! You all heart, huh?"

"We all heart," I said, and we sped on, in the kind of easy understanding that opens at last at the endings of things.

I've heard it said that family is measured not by who comes to the weddings but the funerals. Two weeks after I left the Wests, I got another terse message from my aunt Rose telling me to get on a plane if I could by Sunday. There wasn't any mention of a service, so I had to call her back and ask if it was imminent or—and then I thought of a white sheet coming slowly up, and Grandma Ellen's spotted arms stiffening, and could think of no utterable word for that completion.

"It's all through," she told me.

Before I flew back I called and asked if I could come by and get the severance check Calyph had promised me, as it hadn't appeared in the mail. He didn't pick up, but a few hours later I got a text that read "tomorrow @ 3 good?"

Even this perfunctory summons filled me with a final rush of apprehension and hope, and I was let down to see the check taped to the front door. But when I pulled it off I saw the words "come round back" written on the note line. It was a brisk, windy day, and Calyph was lounging in a tracksuit, leafing through a playbook with his headphones on. I remember it was a silly-looking thing in a three-ring binder, like it was made at Kinko's for a D-III team. He didn't get up, but we shook hands.

"How you been, Jess?"

"My grandmother's died," I told him. I couldn't think of anything else to say. I was standing over him and I wished I could sit. He wouldn't have cared, but it would be taking license to sit without being asked, and I could see myself slumping a little, and then, without thinking of it, making some false little gesture, blinking back tears that weren't coming.

Slowly he shut the book and laid it aside. His immaculate hands seemed careful and sad, and I wondered if he ever really felt anything, in small moments like these when emotion was expected, or if it was just physical grace that made it seem so.

"That's bad," he said. "When'd you last see her?"

"A long time ago. She'd lost her mind," I noted.

"Where is she?"

"Home. Wisconsin. She used to live in Florida a long time."

She'd had an orange tree in her backyard, and there's a picture of me, very young, crawling under this tree and reaching up for the fruit. She liked to tell the story of planting it when I was born so it would grow along with me. When I came eight weeks premature she had the seeds but not the shovel, and she said she had to plant it quick with a broken spade before getting on a plane and coming north to see my mother. The tree seemed much too tall for that, and I suspect it came with the house. She took after me that way.

"Would you fly to Milwaukee?" Calyph asked.

"Unless you need me."

He looked at me kindly. "I never needed you," he said. And then he ran the tips of his fingers over one splayed, pale palm and asked if he could come with me.

"You'd want to do that? It's just my grandmother. I mean, it was time."

He only looked at me, speechless. His eyes widened a little and seemed to get drier. I got the idea he was trying to prevent himself from repeating what I'd said back to me.

"I'd like to see you off," he said finally.

I thanked him. I was grateful, but it was bittersweet. I knew the trip was his way of severing from me with some finality, like maybe if he didn't I'd just stop by and peep in the windows every few weeks because I couldn't help myself. I never could imagine how it was after the trip, after I was gone for good, their second life together with a child on the way and a driver who could keep his distance, full of little gestures of black camaraderie and Antonia walking slower each week. After they were done with me I was done with them. Even being in the same town felt like a burden. Imagining the circuits of their lives entwining invisibly with mine lost its comfort and became a painful reenactment of loss, and before the new year had arrived I'd packed up my things and moved away to Chicago.

To get to my town we had to pass along the shore of Lake Geneva, by the observatory and the stone pillars of old golf courses. Somehow their proud, dated air, a sad pretension in the hot high season, when the place was filled with summer people from Illinois rushing by toward newer courses, seemed almost convincing in the early winter light. Their worn, bald driving ranges and chipped whitewash signs looked like victims of the season only, not of some more enduring slide.

Looking at the mileage signs, I was reminded how seriously the settlers of the area must have taken the idea of future distinction. Radiating out from the lake in every direction were towns with names like Waterford and Avalon, and Harvard, Illinois. That these names of borrowed noblesse lay just down a county road from larger towns like Janesville and Mukwonago, and the Bong State Recreation Area, gave the region its character and made me feel I was almost home. In college I remember telling people that I was from near Lake Geneva, and then adding "the American Lake Geneva" if they seemed confused.

We came up on Fontana, and old brick houses with white

shutters pinned back peered out at us from the shore of the lake through thin, denuded trees.

"Any of those your peoples?" Calyph asked. I think he was getting impatient for the appearance of something that fit my forgeries.

I shook my head. "I might've caddied for some of them," I ventured. "They're probably dead now."

He looked into an open garage as we passed, as though expecting to see the body of an old man laid out on the oil-stained concrete.

What he had or hadn't done with Odette that far-off morning had become, by that point, a sort of permanent uncertainty. I was less certain of his guilt than I'd been when I put the spear to his chest. It's not like I thought him above adultery, but looking down at the cloud floor somewhere over the Dakotas, it occurred to me that if he was innocent, he'd be incapable of telling me so. For Odette to be in his house at all in that thin, gray hour was such a breach of his every code, such a counter to the arrogant uprightness of his every projection of himself, that he'd be every bit as guilty about just having her there as he would about the act itself. Sometimes I thought: She came to call, and he let her come, but when she came, he changed his mind. I imagined her calling him up, on some pretext that in five seconds gave way to the news that the Pharaoh would not marry her. She needed an ear, she would say, or a shoulder, and he knew he would have to supply too that third thing she need not mention—but how could he not let her come?

The slip would have made him seem so small to himself that it'd be preferable to pretend to have gone through with the infidelity and have his measure of guilty fuckery, because to have come so low without the stained trophy of sex to show for it would have been worse yet. I mean, maybe they did, surely they did; the Pharaoh sure thought he had something to avenge. My heart flops around for a way to justify the man, for any sloppy rationalization at all. Still, if they had, I tell myself it must have been long before I arrived, or in some other corner of the house, because I remembered the smell of Shida's room, and the room I found Calyph sleeping in, it did not smell that way; it was pristine.

A little while after we passed the lakeshore houses we came finally into Walworth. We were halfway through before we were there at all. When I guided him onto our street, I saw our mythical fall come to life for Calyph in the rusted frames and sagging bumpers of every old Buick on the block. In the yard of a house with a different Packers flag in each of its basement windows, a mastiff was butting a Hot Wheels around in circles in the driveway as a kid sat watching primly from a still trike.

My aunt's house is at the end of a gravel lane, with an old orchard on one side, and its thin trees looked just gnarled and ghostly enough that it might've still been possible for Calyph to believe that some resplendent ruin awaited us. But it was just a clean little brown house, and the only object in decay was the basketball hoop.

Calyph turned the engine off and we sat for a bit in silence.

"So this is how some fallen-ass white people live?" he asked finally.

"Don't ask them about that," I said. "They won't know what you're talking about."

He looked at me warily, but that was the best explanation I could give him, and I opened my door and stepped out onto the drive. My aunt came around the side of the house, wearing a kerchief and a loud fall jacket.

"I was just doing some raking," she said brusquely, extending Calyph a small, work-softened hand. "I'm Rose Lauren." When he gave his name she nodded shortly, and repeated it back to him without a hitch. Then she hugged me for exactly as long as it took her to tighten her arms one time. We went inside, and she held the door for Calyph with barely a glance. She took him so much in stride I wondered if she was paying attention.

My aunt's is a small-roomed house, brown inside and out, and of course I was looking at it through Calyph's eyes. The kitchen used to smell like dry cat food, but that was gone now, though the cats still remained, lazing on chairs and warming the place. We went from room to room and had a little tour. In the living room Calyph bent to look at the framed picture of my uncle with Robin Yount, and one of the cats leapt across the room to collapse on his foot. He lifted the little thing with one hand and set it backward over his shoulder with an abstracted air. When we went into my old room and I saw my aunt had returned it to its childhood condition, old basketball posters and all, I could only stare into the cat's depthless eyes in mortification.

"J. R. Rider, huh? Wassup, Sheed," Calyph said to the wall.

"You shouldn't have, Rose," I said, and she and Calyph turned to one another and laughed.

"Have you lived here long?" he asked her.

"I've lived here all my life," she said.

In the funeral parlor I was disappointed that my family snuck so few looks at Calyph. But, then, I hadn't accounted for how proud we were, and I'd forgotten how in the presence of death petty curiosities seem to have a spiritual penalty. For his part, he did what he could to blend in, wearing a suit so austere he'd have had to actually scuff it up to make its fineness any less apparent. If people did look, their gazes seemed to settle without great change in expression on me. I'd been away awhile.

When I approached the casket and saw the still, wax face of

my grandmother, and the crushed-paper look of her throat, I had an unbidden memory of her sitting at a glass table, peeling clementines and cussing out the ones with obstinate rinds. Returning to the parlor from this memory, I didn't know what to do with my hands at all, and longed for a ritual, any ritual. I knelt and made the sign of the cross and felt my paralysis loosen under the rote dignity of these formal gestures. I didn't believe in them, but with my hands on the rail I thought of all the proud, old, and corrupted cultures that ritualized their grief fervently and often, and how weak all the rest of us were next to them.

'   As we stood outside, preparing to make the processional, the first breaks in the family formality appeared. People shook hands in a relieved way, and I felt that mingled sense of warmth and danger at being among those who might be reverting to their natural selves. My uncle Ron, who is not an uncle at all, was the first to come over. He'd been among the pallbearers, and seemed enlivened by the task.

"Honored to have you," he said, shaking both our hands. He asked where I'd been living, and repeated "all the way from Orry-gone" twice in an impressed voice.

"Have I seen you before, sir?" he asked Calyph. "Did you go to Carolina?"

"I did."

"I thought so. I'm a Badger man, and you gave it to us pretty good in the tournament a few years back."

"I guess we did," Calyph said.

"Even Krakkenhofer couldn't guard you. Devin Harris, though—what a player he was! Did you know he's in the NBA now?"

"Is he."

"New Jersey Nets! What are you doing these days?" Uncle Ron's face shone with the relish of this questioning, and he put his hand on the crown of his houndstooth hat as though to protect it from a stray gust.

"Just trying to get my knee right."

"Well, you'll always have the college days," my uncle said loudly. Tamping down his hat in a sort of bow, he turned suddenly away.

By the time we settled around the grave site, my family looked familiar at last. With their dark suits and restrained, formalized manners, they could have been almost anyone—even who I'd said they were. But it was a cold day, and the topcoats had got buried beneath parkas, and the severe coiffure beneath ragged knit hats. One of my great-uncles shivered defiantly in his funeral wear until he was taken aside and induced to pull an ancient Bucks headband out of his pocket with trembling hands. When he put it on he looked a fitting patriarch, and though I could read nothing in Calyph's face, I think it was clear we'd never been heirs to anything but spirit and dirt.

Then I looked up and saw a man coming toward us from the middle of the yard. His gray face was weathered, but I could not say his age. A watch chain descended glimmering from his pocket, and his shoes, muddied already at their edges from the earth between the graves, shone at their tops as though they'd just been released from the rag. His face was proud and stern, and he was coming forward in long strides, staring ahead of him all the time.

I thought he might blow right through us, all our huddled circle, and go right to grave's edge. He moved with that kind of scorn, but as he reached the first mourners he stopped abruptly. He was directly across the circle from me and it was impossible to say if he was staring at me or just looking out with strange intensity at all he saw. I would've liked to look away. His was not a calm, wise face; it was not full of easy wisdom nor august wryness nor good humor; it was like no face of age I'd seen. It was full of challenge and vitality. He looked like he wanted to seize something and drink it and throw down the glass. Sometimes I have seen old men, men who have made a standard for what a full life means and achieved it, and even if their standards are laughable and their lives are all wrong, their eyes are yet full of hot, intolerable light. Smug, limited men, driving terrible cars, checking their gaudy watches, commanding steak for lunch and eating it like they would jam their knife into the very eye of death, the fulfillment pours off them anyhow, like liquid gold. This man, he looked like those men, and yet he was still not satisfied. He had a look of hunger, of wishing even now for more life, and of barely suppressed rage at having to do with less. As he looked at me—and he must have been looking at me, I felt them all around me then, all the family I had made—I felt the familiar, scouring feeling of being looked at by someone at once younger and older than myself. That feeling is pure humility, and I'd been given it by Calyph and Antonia and all the betters whose memories tease me even now with casual recollections of a dry, ageless laugh or an immaculate hand flash, filling me with the white exultant jealousy I love so well it feels like love itself. Then the man pulled the watch from his pocket and flipped it open, and the bittersweet look on his face intensified, as though he were delighting in something seen in the dial, and at the same time cursing, how late, how late, and then he stepped to the side and was gone and I was alone again with my real family, who were here and there bashfully holding hands in their mittens and gloves, and I put my hands into my empty pockets, wishing I had brought something ratty of my own to wear.

After the funeral we went back to my aunt's for a meal. There was a honey ham and there were meatballs with grape jelly and brandy old-fashioneds, and since the meal was eaten in the afternoon it felt like a holiday, an informal one where the uncles were allowed to bring a can of beer to the table. Afterward there were even presents. It was the birthday of a thin, black-haired boy who must have been a distant cousin and who liked to lift up his shirt and suck in his stomach until his ribs bulged out.

"Not at the table, Travis—my God!" his mother said.

"I'm from the Sudan," the boy said proudly. He was just young enough not to be punished for this in public and probably he knew it.

"Travis is six today," his mother said, directing a shamed look halfway down the spread, near Calyph's plate. "He doesn't know better."

"I'm seven," Travis said.

"He's six," his mother repeated desperately. "If he was seven we'd have to shoot him."

Then the presents were over, and people were slipping away. As the grid of cars filling the drive loosened, we heard a light rhythmic thudding from outside, interspersed every few seconds with a heavier sound.

The noise brought Travis's head up from where he'd been dragging the edges of his plate for cake frosting. "I want to play," he said, to no one in particular, and then his empty chair was rocking slightly side-to-side and his mother was calling without confidence for him to come back.

Outside, a couple of neighborhood boys were shooting at the rim with an old ball. Travis was hounding them and chasing the rebounds. When Calyph followed me out, they all just stopped. Even the birthday boy stood awed. It was as though Calyph had only now become a six-nine black man who wore a gravely resplendent suit and whose hands moved too quickly even when he was doing something so minute as reaching for his napkin.

One of the boys shot a self-conscious air ball and they all ran after it ravenously. Someone else snatched it up and passed it to Calyph. He turned the ball in his hands, feeling the worn grain, then passed it softly back.

Immediately it came back to him.

"Can you dunk?" one of the boys asked.

"Look at his leg," his friend whispered loudly. "It's messed up."

"Shoot," Travis urged. "Shoot."

Calyph looked down at the ball. Time had smoothed it and drained it of its color, and the leather was peeling a little in places. It was the kind of ball that looked like it ought to have been held by a man in spectacles and tiny shorts in an old photograph.

He lifted the ball for a second, and gave a grimace of a smile. Then he put it down on his hip. The hoop was maybe twenty feet away. The kids were staring at him, waiting. We all waited, to see if he would shoot. I looked into his face and saw that his eyes were narrow and inward-seeing. What if he missed? I think we all considered the ball's spinning, soundless drop through the tattered net an inevitable conclusion. But he was injured, and though his new contract was still good, he could have been traded any day to a team that might have tried to get him to retire for cap relief; at any time his place could have been taken by younger men who smiled benignly for the fans and made no trouble, who might in a single game have declared a talent that rendered his own second-rate and expendable. And if he did miss, who knew the judgment that would come from my skeletal cousin from the Sudan?

Finally he lifted the ball. Then he put his other arm over his face, covering his eyes with the crook of his elbow. Careless and blind, he heaved the thing like a baseball toward the backboard. It hit with a tremendous crash, slipped through the net on the carom, and hit my cousin on the side of the head. Instantly he began to cry.

Calyph swore exultantly. "You ain't hurt!" he called down, laughing.

He took my shoulder and lowered his voice to a whisper. It seemed a needless intimacy, and once more I was thrilled and terrified. "Clean this up for me, J, for once in your life," he said softly, and then he turned and went into the house.

I went over to Travis and put my hand awkwardly around his shoulders, pretending to examine him. Sure enough, as soon as Calyph was gone he stopped crying and his eyes took on a sly look.

"Tell on him," he urged. "Tell them he hurt me."

"Wasn't that fun?"

"That guy's mean."

"He's all right," I said.

"No," he told me definitely. "They're just for TV. They're cool on TV. In real life they're dicks."

I nodded at him sagely, for I could see that this, too, was a put-on, that he was after all glad to be hit, and so to be the center of things once more. I think he'd even leaned into the path of the ball a little.

I felt him twisting in my grasp, the young life of him straining to be free.

"I never want to meet another one," he said fiercely.

"You will," I said, and when I did, it seemed, for the first time, the voicing of a slightly tired feeling that would soon run its course, and then I would be on to something else, and be new again once more, and then I let my cousin go, and watched him run off through the freezing grass to tell the story to everyone.

ACKNOWLEDGMENTS

Thanks, first and foremost, to Lan Samantha Chang, Chris Parris-Lamb, and Barry Harbaugh, the three people who most changed my life as a writer and made this book possible.

Thanks also to the Michener-Copernicus Society of America and everyone at the Iowa Writers' Workshop, particularly Connie Brothers.

Thanks to all my friends, especially early readers Katie Chase, Matthew Flaming, Tom Macher, Jennifer duBois, Maggie Shipstead, Nimo Johnson, Katie Perry, and Diana Wilson. Thanks to Sarah Karon, Matty Griffin, Jason Lewis, Kevin Gonzalez, Ben Hale, Alex Perez, and Lucas Bernhart for seeing me through good times and bad in Iowa City, and to Rebecca Jean Olson, Matt Tamura, Jay Leary, Jordan Dykstra, and Cooper Cruz for seeing me through better times and worse in Portland.

ABOUT THE AUTHOR

Chris Leslie-Hynan is originally from Wisconsin and received his MFA in fiction from the Iowa Writers' Workshop in 2008. He lives in Portland, Oregon. This is his first book.